An Everlasting Smile

Dali Publishing

Synopsis

A journey through growing up and growing emotionally and spiritually. Charting several relationships and how they impact on Adam and those around him. Thought provoking, funny and poignant.

Adam is growing up in London with contrasting drivers to his character. On the positive side he has charm, humour, good looks and is quite creative. On the down side he comes from a rough area, endures a terrible home and school life, has no stable influences and is prone to dream and drift. The constant through his childhood and into adulthood is the juxtaposition of confidence/bravado versus insecurity/self-doubt. His decisions and reasoning are ruled by whichever of these is prevalent at any given time.

Set in London, The Greek Islands and Sydney.

<u>Characters</u>

Adam: From London. Schoolboy to mid-20s. Charming, attractive, funny, but insecure. The confidence he portrays is not always real. The decisions he makes are reflective of the belief/non-belief in himself and may seem puzzling to those who see the image rather than the heart of him.

Eleonore: From Paris. 4 years older than Adam. Beautiful, intelligent, driven, sophisticated. Much more worldly wise than Adam. Meets Adam when he's 18 and she's 22. Very emotional. Like Adam, wears her heart on her sleeve.

Tim: Adam's best friend from London, same age as Adam. Kind, loyal, responsible, wise. Often called upon to help Adam.

Grace: Early 30s. Bohemian, seemingly carefree, very nice girl next door with a secret she doesn't want to reveal to Adam. Wants to be close to Adam. Unclear if the relationship is envisioned as platonic. They have an instant connection.

Zoe: Similar age to Adam. Wild, hedonistic, weary and cynical because of being treated badly by men. Wants to be loved and seeks to hide her unhappiness in partying and being promiscuous. The dark to Grace's light.

Mr & Mrs Garnier: 50s. Eleonore's parents. Traditional, close-knit French family. Eleonore's brother died when she was very young and they are now very protective of their daughter, particularly Mr Garnier.

Dhara: 20s. Friendly, funny, deputy to Eleonore at work. Sees things simplistically. Big heart.

Olivia: Late 20s, Tim's girlfriend. Caring, loving, but also demanding. Wants marriage and a family.

Vincenzo: 50s. Italian origin. Grace's neighbour. Lives with his wife. Very protective of Grace.

Miles and Regan: Late 20s early 30s. Macho lads at the sports warehouse where Adam works. Miles slightly more perceptive than Regan.

Red: late 50s/60s. Adam' s boss. Quite, philosophical, dry humour.

Paul: Late 30s. Helps Eleonore in her new role. Wants to be close to her. Very nice, sincere, well-educated, all-round good man.

Greg: 50s. Australian business man. Confident, successful and persuasive. Runs the business in London and Sydney. His brother (who we don't see) is the silent partner.

Teagan: Early 40s. Greg's sister-in-law. Director in Sydney. Not much ability but married to Greg's brother and can seemingly do whatever she likes. Takes an instant jealous dislike to Eleonore.

Miss Carmen: Adam's French teacher. Subject of schoolboy fantasies.

Maxwell, Gareth, Patrick, Jack: Children Adam interacts with while at school.

Bethany: 20s. Chinese. Works at coffee/ice cream bar in Portobello Road, near Adam's apartment.

Local man/musician in Ios: 30s/40s Greek/European.

Street trader: 40s. From London.

Cab driver: 40s-50s. From London.

Katie: 30s. From Australia, Greg's PA.

An Everlasting Smile

Andre Cristelli

britalian@zoho.com
+44 7760298698

EXT. HOUSING ESTATE - DAY

A run-down housing estate in South London. Adam as a small
child, is about to attend his first day at an unruly London
primary school, receiving advice from a local boy, Maxwell.
He's in the year above and lives in the next block to Adam.

                    MAXWELL
          Sometime this week Gareth Hinds and
          Patrick Ashton are gonna put your
          head in the toilet, hold it there and
          flush. Hopefully, it will just be
          water. If they don't do that, they'll
          get you in the playground by the bins
          and make you get on your knees.
          Gareth is bigger and stronger but
          Patrick is a maniac. They'll tell you
          they're gonna kick the crap out of
          you if you don't kiss their boots.
          Whatever happens, do not kiss their
          boots!

                    ADAM
          You just said they'll kick the crap
          out of me if I don't.

                    MAXWELL
          It's likely they will either way, but
          if you kiss their boots they'll pick
          on you every day. You'll have the
          next four years of…hell.

EXT. SCHOOL PLAYGROUND - DAY

School at break time. Adam is in the playground, finds
himself in the vicinity of the bins. He doesn't see them
coming, turns around and Gareth and Patrick are smiling at
him.

They usher him behind the wall of the bin chamber out of
sight of the teacher on duty in the playground.

                    GARETH
          Get on your knees.

                    PATRICK
          Do it. Now!

Adam gets on his knees, looking at them both as he does.

                    PATRICK
          Kiss my boots.

Adam shakes his head but doesn't speak.

>GARETH
>I would do what he says if I was you.

>ADAM
>I don't think you would.

>PATRICK
>Do you know who we are?

Adam is shaking, clearly petrified.

>ADAM
>I'm not scared.

>GARETH
>You've got five seconds.

>ADAM
>I'm not very good at maths.

>PATRICK
>We're gonna start counting, if you
>don't kiss my boots…

>ADAM
>Can I have nineteen seconds?

>GARETH & PATRICK
>What?

>ADAM
>Nineteen. It's my lucky number.
>Please. Then I'll do it. Kiss your
>boots. Are they clean?

>PATRICK
>Start counting then.

Adam counts very slowly. Gets to eleven and stops.

>ADAM
>Sorry, lost count.

>GARETH
>Twelve. Carry on.

>ADAM
>OK, nearly half way there.

Adam counts even slower, from twelve to eighteen, then the bell rings, Gareth and Patrick look up and Adam runs towards the school building.

INT. SCHOOL - DAY

We see him sitting at his desk, still shaking but smiling with joy at the same time.

EXT. STREET - DAY

After school he sees Maxwell on the walk home.

                    ADAM
          Maxwell.

                    MAXWELL
          How was your first day?

                    ADAM
          They caught me.

                    MAXWELL
          Already. Toilet or bins?

                    ADAM
          Bins.

                    MAXWELL
          Did you?

                    ADAM
          No.

                    MAXWELL
          What did they do to you?

                    ADAM
          Nothing. I realised something today.

                    MAXWELL
          What?

                    ADAM
          How to win at 100 metres.

                    MAXWELL
          You might need a bit more than 100
          metres. Anyway, well done.

SUPERIMPOSE: Four years later

EXT/INT. SCHOOL - DAY

Adam is standing outside the new secondary school. A very
large inner London school, known for being very rough. 1700
boys, almost all male teachers. He is not looking forward to
his first day.

He endures three lessons with sarcastic and sadistic male
teachers, while thinking about home, where last night he
endured his mother throwing a china cup at his father and it
becoming lodged in his father's head.

He listens to the aggressive teacher while still thinking
about home. A pneumatic drill is heard outside.

The bell rings and he is now walking slowly to his next
class.

He is pushed by an older child who then runs off. A teacher
walks by and shouts at him to get off the floor. The
pneumatic drill outside is getting louder.

The next lesson is French and the teacher is one of the very
few female teachers at the school, Miss Carmen.

                    MISS CARMEN
          Settle down boys. Today, you start a
          journey, which if you focus and work
          hard at it, may become very
          beneficial to your future.

Adam is mesmerized, so much so he doesn't pay much attention
to the lesson content. The lesson is about to end.

                    MISS CARMEN
          Let's recap on the new vocabulary.
          What is the French word for artist?
          Adam?

                    ADAM
          Artista.

                    MISS CARMEN
          Adam, it's French not Italian.

The boys in class laugh at Adam as the bell rings.

                    MISS CARMEN
          Please learn the new vocabulary to a
          proficient level in time for the next
          lesson.

EXT. STREET - DAY

Adam is walking home and sees a friend (two years older) from a different school who lives on the estate, Jack.

                    JACK
          How's that horrible school?

                    ADAM
          Alright Jack. I wish I was at yours.

                    JACK
          Mine's not great, but yours…

                    ADAM
          It does have one good point.

                    JACK
          Yeah?

                    ADAM
          Her name's Miss Carmen. I am never
          gonna forget her, as long as I live.
          She is perfect.

                    JACK
          Is she older than you?

                    ADAM
          She's the French teacher.

                    JACK
          Is she French?

                    ADAM
          I don't know, but when she speaks,
          it's like she's saying things to me
          in another language.

                    JACK
          She is.

                    ADAM
          No, I mean, it's a language only her
          and me know.

                    JACK
          You're in love with your French
          teacher, got it. Well, mine is a fat,
          sweaty old west country bastard with
          bad breath who hasn't even mastered

                    English yet. At least if you do
                    transfer to my school he'll be safe
                    from your pre-teenage lust.

INT. ADAM'S BEDROOM - NIGHT

That night Adam is lying in bed fantasising about the future.

DREAM - INT. GRAND HOUSE - NIGHT

Miss Carmen is sitting in a grand house by a roaring log fire
marking books.

An older Adam walks in the room. He says something in French,
she corrects him and tells him he'll have to stay the night
until he is perfect.

END OF DREAM.

EXT. STREET - ONE YEAR LATER

Adam meets Jack again.

                    JACK
               How's it going? How's Miss Coleman?

                    ADAM
               Miss Carmen.

                    JACK
               If you like.

                    ADAM
               She is getting married, to Mr Baines,
               the geography teacher. He's boring,
               and a bit ugly.

                    JACK
               Did you expect she was going to wait
               for you?

                    ADAM
               Well.

                    JACK
               Just move on. Your sexy French
               teacher has had geography, now she's
               history.

INT. SCHOOL - DAY

It's now the last day of school, as Adam is leaving he passes
the now Mrs Baines in the corridor.

                    ADAM
          Hello Miss Carmen.

                    MRS BAINES
          Hello Adam. You know that hasn't been
          my name for a long time.

                    ADAM
          Yes miss. I'm leaving today.

                    MRS BAINES
          Indeed, lots of you are. Which
          college are you going to?

                    ADAM
          I'm not.

                    MRS BAINES
          Oh, do you have an apprenticeship?

                    ADAM
          I'm going to get a job.

                    MRS BAINES
          Doing what?

                    ADAM
          I don't know yet.

                    MRS BAINES
          Adam, try and get some focus, some
          direction. Think about what you
          really want, and be true to yourself.
          Your bravado will only take you so
          far.
          Eventually you'll have to live in the
          reality the rest of us inhabit. It's
          not so bad.

Mr Baines approaches and takes his wife's bag. He nods at
Adam.

As they are walking away she slightly stumbles. He helps her
as she smiles lovingly.

We then see Adam looking at the school for the last time.
Some boys who are leaving the school are burning their
blazers.

Adam looks at his, thinks for a moment, but doesn't join in.

EXT. STREET - DAY

We see him walking home alone.

INT. JOBCENTRE - DAY

Adam sits before a consultant.

                    CONSULTANT
          What about this one? It's local. The
          pay isn't great but you can work your
          way up.

                    ADAM
          I don't understand what it is.

                    CONSULTANT
          It's a magazine that specialises
          in foreign travel. How good are
          you at geography?

                    ADAM
          I have bad memories of geography,
          preferred French.

                    CONSULTANT
          Your choice.

                    ADAM
          Ok, can you put me forward?

                    CONSULTANT
          I spoke to the manager earlier,
          they're interviewing tomorrow. Have
          you got a suit?

                    ADAM
          Yes.

INT. ADAM'S HOUSE - MORNING

We see Adam unpicking the badge from his black school
blazer. He puts some dark trousers on but it is clear he
isn't wearing a proper suit.

INT. INTERVIEW'S LOCATION - DAY

He's now waiting to go into the interview obviously
nervous but trying to convince himself he's confident. He
goes into the toilets and combs his hair and speaks to
himself.

                    ADAM
          Well done. You were awesome! You got
          the job.

He notices some stitching of the school badge remaining on
the blazer.

He quickly rips it out but that leaves a small tear in the
fabric.

                    INTERVIEWER 1
          Hello Adam, how are you today?

                    ADAM
          I'm good thank you. You?

                    INTERVIEWER 2
          Adam, what do you know about travel,
          other countries, other cultures?

                    ADAM
          I'm very keen to learn.

                    INTERVIEWER 2
          Have you travelled at all?

                    ADAM
          We had school trips.

                    INTERVIEWER 1
          Where have you visited?

Adam has never been abroad but doesn't want to lie this early
in the interview.

                    ADAM
          There was a school trip to France.
          And when I was younger my family went
          to Italy.

Adam is content, as he hasn't said he's been to France or
Italy.

                    INTERVIEWER 1
          Anywhere outside of Europe?

                    ADAM
          Not yet. But I'm hoping.

Adam is now starting to lose the false confidence he
convinced himself he had as he catches Interviewer 2 looking
at his clothes.

                    INTERVIEWER 1
          Is Mumbai east or west of India?

                    ADAM
          East.

                    INTERVIEWER 1
          West.

                    ADAM
          Yes of course, west. I mean, India is
          in the east.

                    INTERVIEWER 2
          Why are you wearing a school blazer
          to an interview?

FLASHBACK - INT/EXT. VARIOUS - DAY

- Adam flashes back to the poor living conditions at home -
The bullying at school - The pneumatic drill

END OF FLASHBACK.

INT. INTERVIEW'S LOCATION - DAY

Adam starts to be visibly uncomfortable, but then somehow
composes himself. He speaks with apparent confidence and
eloquence.

                    ADAM
          I'll be totally honest; I didn't
          expect the interview to be arranged
          so quickly. My suit is in the dry
          cleaner's, I was hoping to put back
          the interview until tomorrow so I
          could collect it. I really want to
          learn about the travel business and
          I've heard so many great things about
          this company. I had to weigh up the
          likelihood of you appointing someone
          else before seeing me, against
          turning up here dressed more
          appropriately. I might have made the
          wrong call, probably have. If I could

do it again, …my dress sense can improve, obviously, but you're not going to find anyone as committed and dedicated as I'll be, I think that might make the difference, to the company, wouldn't you think?

                    INTERVIEWER 1
          Thank you. We're not looking for a
          CEO at the moment, just an office
          junior.

                    INTERVIEWER 2
          Have you got any questions for us?

                    ADAM
          Has Mumbai always been in the west?

Adam smiles at them. One of them looks at the itinerary for the interviews, Adam is second to last and the last candidate has "cancelled". The other interviewer smiles, seemingly amused with Adam.

                    INTERVIEWER 1
          We'll make a decision by the end of
          the day.

EXT. STREET - DAY

Adam is walking home. He takes off the blazer and puts it in a rubbish bin adjacent to a bus stop even though it is pouring with rain. On the bus some children are coming home from his old school. On seeing this they start banging on the window and cheering.

INT. ADAM'S HOUSE - DAY

Adam is now at home listening to music and looking out the window, very wet with a towel around his neck. He is thinking about his unhappy childhood, unhappy school life and unhappy home environment.

The phone rings. He is shocked to be offered the job. The rain stops and the sun comes out.

INT/EXT. SPORTS WAREHOUSE - DAY

Adam is now being interviewed again, this time at a giant sports warehouse.

He walks out of the building and his friend Tim sees him as

he's driving by. Tim stops. Adam gets in the car.

                    TIM
          What are you doing?

                    ADAM
          I just went for a job.

                    TIM
          Have you left the magazine?

                    ADAM
          I think the senior management and
          me had differing views on the
          direction the company should be
          taking.

Tim laughs.

                    TIM
          Hopefully at this interview they
          didn't ask you if London is in the
          north or the south.

                    ADAM
          Actually, the guy liked me. Offered
          me the job there and then. You like
          tennis don't you?

                    TIM
          Are those two sentences related or is
          this you further perfecting the art
          of changing the subject to avoid any
          embarrassing revelations?

                    ADAM
          He's called Red. He's as old as
          Shakespeare, with the same hairstyle,
          but he's alright. He used to string
          for Wimbledon champions, still does
          for the England number 1. He's gonna
          teach me.

                    TIM
          What?

                    ADAM
          Tennis racquet stringing.

                    TIM
          From globetrotting travel writer to
          stringing tennis racquets. Are you
          sure?

                    ADAM
          It pays more. 50% more.

                    TIM
          Maths was never your strong point.

                    ADAM
          I know, I was always better at French.

                    TIM
          In your dreams.

                    ADAM
          Yeah, too often.

INT. SPORTS WAREHOUSE - DAY

We see Adam being trained by Red. Red can expertly string a
tennis racquet in 15 minutes, while making coffee at the same
time.

After an hour of focus and just when Adam thinks he's
reaching the climax of his first work of art, he looks down
in horror to see one of the cross strings going over instead
of under. This probably happened over half an hour ago and
cannot be fixed, even by the trusty hands of Red. Adam has
to start again and Red makes another coffee.

Outside in the warehouse there are two floors of activity.
On the very cold ground floor are the lads, the packing crew
with their humour and camaraderie.

On the very warm first floor are the offices. Apart from the
brothers who own the company these offices are staffed mostly
by young women.

Separating the two floors are very dangerous looking metal
steps and even through the deafening music the sound of heels
navigating those steps always seems to permeate.

We see a couple of these first-floor women, who seem to dread
the prospect of coming down to the warehouse floor, because
after conquering the sometimes-slippery steps, they'll be
faced with the "banter" of the lads.

Miles and Regan are the comedy duo in the warehouse.
Confident and assured.

                    MILES
How's it going Adam? Is Red showing
you the tricks of the trade?

                    ADAM
I think he's despairing of me. I
haven't yet got the knack.

                    REGAN
As long as you've got the knack for
other things.

                    ADAM
Maybe.

                    MILES
I think Jade's got her eye on you.

                    ADAM
Which one is Jade?

                    MILES
The pretending to be shy one.

                    REGAN
Medium/Short brown hair.

                    MILES
She's a bit wild. Can you handle her?

                    ADAM
I'm sure it will be easier than
stringing racquets.

                    REGAN
If you're not good with your hands…

                    MILES
It would be fun to see her boyfriend
annoyed and jealous.

                    REGAN
He has violent tendencies.

                    MILES
Have you seen how he waits for her
after work and looks around to see if
any men are looking at her when she
leaves?

                    ADAM
          I should get back.

                    REGAN
          Don't worry about him, we'll be there
          mate.

                    MILES
          But Jade's only a B. B plus at
          most. You can't risk your pretty
          face on a B.

                    ADAM
          I can risk it for an A can I?

                    REGAN
          There's only one A. Her name begins
          with E and she's French.

                    ADAM
          I know. French was always my
          favourite subject at school.

                    MILES
          You fancy your chances with her do
          you?

                    ADAM
          Definitely not.

                    REGAN
          This boy's not stupid Miles.

At that moment the E to which Regan referred, appears at the
top of the stairs. She is the Finance Manager, Eleonore. She
saunters down the precarious metal steps in heels with
complete confidence.

Adam sees through the window in the service department where
he works out to the warehouse.

Regan and Miles try to taunt her and she says something to
them which embarrasses and quietens them.

Adam smiles and goes back to work in case Eleonore sees him
as she walks past. He is trying to work faster but clearly
struggling.

Eleonore smiles as she passes.

INT. SPORTS WAREHOUSE - DAY

Over the next couple of weeks Adam is becoming more immersed in the lad culture at the warehouse. In the company of Miles and Regan he is comfortable and seemingly confident. However, not so much that he has yet summoned up the power to say hello to Eleonore. He sees Miles during a break.

                    ADAM
          How old is she?

                    MILES
          Who?

                    ADAM
          The French goddess.

                    MILES
          Something like 22 or 23 I think. A
          bit mature for you?

                    ADAM
          Four years.

                    MILES
          I wouldn't worry about the age
          difference too much Adam.

                    ADAM
          Why?

                    MILES
          It's not like anything's gonna happen.

                    ADAM
          Has she got a boyfriend?

                    MILES
          According to Regan, she dumped the
          last guy.

                    ADAM
          Do you know why?

                    MILES
          No. Anyway, enough of the questions,
          lascivious lad. You'll have the
          opportunity to ask her on Friday
          night.

                    ADAM
          What's happening on Friday night?

                    MILES
          Jade's leaving.

                    ADAM
          Yeah I knew that, but how does that
          get me more informed about my future
          wife.

                    MILES
          Regan! Come here. Adam's gonna marry
          Eleonore.

                    ADAM
          Shhh!

                    MILES
          She can't hear above the music.

                    REGAN
          Well Adam, as you know, I like a
          little bet now and again, but I would
          more likely bet on Christmas
          happening in June, not at the end of
          this month, before I laid money on
          you and Eleonore getting together. No
          offence.

                    ADAM
          Offence definitely taken.

                    MILES
          Jade's leaving party, Friday night at
          Kelly's, you're invited. Your future
          wife will be there. Good luck!

INT. KELLY'S WINE BAR - EVENING

After going home to change, Adam tentatively enters the
premises and for no apparent reason half dances towards the
bar.

As he is ordering a drink a look of disbelief is witnessed on
the faces of a couple of the warehouse lads next to him. They
look at Adam, then behind him, then at him again. Adam is
imagining Staying Alive is playing and picturing everyone in
disco attire. He then sees a psychedelic ray of light in a
white dress emanating from behind him.

As he turns around Eleonore grabs his arm and pulls him onto the makeshift dance floor.

We see outside thunder and lightning, while Adam sees before him oceans of dazzling sunshine, Eleonore.

After the dance Regan pounces on Adam, closely followed by Miles.

                    REGAN
          Are you taking Eleonore home?

                    MILES
          If anything happens later, we want a
          full report and a rating. Don't
          disappoint!

Eleonore remains on the dance floor for a long time with other women from the office until she disappears with Dhara, the assistant manager to Eleonore.

Meanwhile Adam is having a few drinks to help summon up some courage.

                    DHARA
          So, Adam!

                    ELEONORE
          He's cute. A bit young for me.

                    DHARA
          That won't mean a thing when you're
          both a couple of years older.

                    ELEONORE
          So he's going to age and I'll stay
          the same, until he catches up?

                    DHARA
          No dear, I'm just saying. My father
          is twelve years older than my mother.

                    ELEONORE
          And they're happy?

                    DHARA
          No. Hate each other. Just going
          through a divorce.

                    ELEONORE
          Thanks for that.

                    DHARA
He was looking up the meaning of your
name.

                    ELEONORE
Your father?

                    DHARA
Adam! Regan mentioned it to Jade. You
know what that means don't you?

                    ELEONORE
That you all gossip when you should
be working.

Eleonore smiles and Dhara leads her back to the dance floor.
Adam keeps looking up to see if he can get to speak to
Eleonore alone.

Eventually, she makes her way to the bar, at which point Adam
intercepts her.

                    ADAM
Hey shining light. That's what your
name, apparently means?

                    ELEONORE
It can mean that but it depends where
you are finding the translation.

                    ADAM
I don't remember, but you are
definitely the shining light at work.

                    ELEONORE
You don't know what I'm like out of
work though.

                    ADAM
I'd like to know. I wonder if I'm
going to.

                    ELEONORE
Oui, peut-être. Some of the girls are
going to a club after we leave here.
They want me to go. Shall I?

                    ADAM
That doesn't seem, you are not the
type to ask a man what she should do.

                    ELEONORE
Oh type, interesting, you know I'm a
shining light and now you know my
type it seems!

                    ADAM
I don't know anything about you
Eleonore. You work upstairs, doing I
have no idea what, and you come down
to…

                    ELEONORE
You're right Adam, you don't
know anything about me and I
know less about you.

                    ADAM
Can there be less than not knowing
anything?

                    ELEONORE
Prouver que j'ai raison serait
admettre que je puisse avoir tort.

                    ADAM
You must know I didn't understand a
word of that. It sounded great!

                    ELEONORE
Proving that I am right could be
admitting that I could be wrong. It's
a quote from Pierre Augustin Caron de
Beaumarchais. Do you know him?

                    ADAM
Not yet.

                    ELEONORE
He was a spy, politician, publisher,
arms-dealer, musician, inventor,
watchmaker, revolutionary, supported
the French revolution and the
American war of independence, wrote
several plays including The Marriage
of Figaro which Mozart based the
opera on.

                    ADAM
Wow!

                    ELEONORE
          Also he married three times and some
          people think he poisoned his first
          two wives. They were both from
          wealthy families.

                    ADAM
          Amazing!

                    ELEONORE
          What part?

                    ADAM
          All of it really.

                    ELEONORE
          Murdering his wives?

                    ADAM
          I think, if you do as much as he did,
          some mistakes are inevitable.

                    ELEONORE
          Are we going somewhere, or am I going
          with the girls?

                    ADAM
          We're going somewhere.

EXT. BAR - CONTINUOUS

We see Eleonore leave the bar quietly and Adam is waiting
around the corner.

EXT. COVENT GARDEN - NIGHT

We then see them in Central London, Covent Garden, having a
lot of fun, drinking eating, watching street performers,
laughing heartily and looking at each other a lot. Adam is
putting his coat around Eleonore as she kisses him.

We then see them flagging a cab. Eleonore is telling the
driver her address and then whispering something to him.
Adam, intoxicated on alcohol and Eleonore, doesn't notice.

EXT. ELEONORE'S APARTMENT - NIGHT

The cab is now stopping outside Eleonore's apartment and
Eleonore is about to get out as Adam kisses her goodbye.

                    ADAM
          Au revoir, beautiful lady.

Eleonore smiles and slowly walks a few steps towards her
apartment block, then stops to take her shoes off. Adam
speaks to the cab driver.

                    ADAM
          We're heading south now my friend.

                    CAB DRIVER
          Probably not.

                    ADAM
          Oh no. You're not one of these I
          don't go south of the river this time
          of night cabbies are you?

                    CAB DRIVER
          I'm going south of the river. I don't
          think you are.

Eleonore smiles and beckons Adam to follow her to the
apartment.

Adam pays the cab driver and gets out of the cab. The cab
driver smiles and drives away.

Eleonore hands Adam her shoes and puts her arms around him.

                    ELEONORE
          I'm sure you can do all those things
          Pierre Augustin Caron de Beaumarchais
          did, only more, and better.

                    ADAM
          You have a lot of faith in me.

                    ELEONORE
          Is it justified?

                    ADAM
          I hope so.

INT. SPORTS WAREHOUSE - DAY

Monday morning at the sports warehouse: Eleonore is focused
on her work, and so far the other women are resisting the
temptation to ask her what happened on Friday night. Adam is
making Red a coffee and the lads are outside bantering. Miles
gesticulates for him to come out to the warehouse floor.

                    MILES
What happened?

                    ADAM
When?

                    MILES
In 1066, when do you think?

                    ADAM
On the 14th of October there was some
kind of skirmish around Hastings. I
think the Normans came out on top.

                    MILES
What happened? Regan was taking bets.

                    ADAM
What were the shortest odds?

                    MILES
That you tried to get Eleonore back
to your place, or hers. She kicked
your ass. You went home, frustrated!

                    ADAM
That definitely sounds the most
likely outcome, wouldn't you think?
Red needs me. Those racquets won't
string themselves. Although I'm sure
they'd prefer to.

Dhara has been waiting for her moment, and now approaches
Eleonore.

                    DHARA
Everyone wants to know!

                    ELEONORE
We had fun.

                    DHARA
Is that it?

                    ELEONORE
Yes.

                    DHARA
Eleonore, as your deputy I think it
is my responsibility, in the spirit
of providing you support, to make you
a coffee and have a chat.

                    ELEONORE
It was fun. But I'm older than him. I
don't think it's going to happen
again.

                    DHARA
It looked like he was besotted with
you.

                    ELEONORE
Really?

                    DHARA
Where did you go?

                    ELEONORE
Covent Garden, a bar or two, enjoying
the atmosphere.

                    DHARA
And after?

                    ELEONORE
It was lovely.

                    DHARA
So you're seeing him again?

                    ELEONORE
I don't want any gossip.

                    DHARA
You know what Dhara means don't you?
Sustaining and preserving. I'm going
to sustain your happiness and
preserve your reputation.

                    ELEONORE
If I ever have a daughter, Dhara will
be high on my list of possible names.

INT. ADAM'S HOUSE - NIGHT

Later that evening Adam gets a call.

                    ELEONORE
Bonsoir.

                    ADAM
Bonsoir, ma lumière brilliante. (Good evening, my
shining light)

                    ELEONORE
          Oh Impressive! You've been practicing.

                    ADAM
          Yeah that's as far as I've got.
          Perhaps you'll be my new French
          teacher, the last one kind of
          abandoned me.

                    ELEONORE
          Perhaps. I thought you might have
          contacted me today.

                    ADAM
          You told me to be discrete.

                    ELEONORE
          Do you always do as you're told?

                    ADAM
          Define always.

                    ELEONORE
          Always, is how I see us.

                    ADAM
          Wow!

                    ELEONORE
          You give a lot of mixed signals Adam.

                    ADAM
          In what way?

                    ELEONORE
          In every way. There are moments you
          are supremely confident. Then it
          seems it isn't, you know, real.

Adam doesn't speak. Eleonore changes the subject.

                    ELEONORE
          Did the boys say anything?

                    ADAM
          They wanted to know what happened.
          They had a book running, apparently.

                    ELEONORE
          Book?

                    ADAM
Regan was taking bets. The most
popular one being you sent me home.
They think you're much too good for
me. So do I. I think that makes
everyone.

                    ELEONORE
Not quite.

                    ADAM
Well the only other person who might
challenge that wisdom would have been
my grandmother, who sadly died five
years ago. I was her favourite.

                    ELEONORE
So I don't get a say?

                    ADAM
Yes, of course you do.

                    ELEONORE
You're more than good enough. I was
thinking perhaps for you it was just
fun.

                    ADAM
Are you crazy? Eleonore you're
amazing! It was the best weekend of
my life. The thought of more of
those...

                    ELEONORE
Good. I want more.

                    ADAM
Really?

                    ELEONORE
Yes. Adam, it's time to realise, that
when this woman says how she feels,
you can be sure she means it. And
although, thankfully, the age
difference between you and me is not
as great as you and your grandmother,
I also see the things she saw in you.
You are my favourite too.

Over the next short period we see Adam becoming more
confident at work and noticeably more mature than the rest
of the lads. The relationship with Eleonore is discrete but
an open secret to most at work.

INT. BAR - EVENING

Adam is at a bar with Tim and Tim's girlfriend, Olivia.

                    TIM
          Another white wine darling?

                    OLIVIA
          Oh, yes please!

                    TIM
          Ads, Guinness? Or are you graduating
          to the hard stuff now?

                    OLIVIA
          No he isn't! Eleonore's not here. No
          getting him drunk. Well, not yet.

                    TIM
          Looking forward to meeting her mate,
          how long has it been now?

                    ADAM
          Well let's see. Jade's leaving drink
          was on that Friday night, by Saturday
          morning I lost part of my vision, so
          I'm unable to see any other women, by
          Sunday evening I was commencing the
          learning of seriously rude French
          vocab, by Monday I was lying to work
          colleagues, yeah it's been about…

Eleonore walks in looking stunningly attractive. Adam looks
at her, clearly spellbound.

                    ADAM
          Forever.

Eleonore kisses Adam and meets Tim and Olivia for the first
time.

                    TIM
          Eleonore! It's great to finally meet
          you.

                    OLIVIA
Hello Eleonore, Olivia.

                    ELEONORE
At last! We're in the company
of people we don't work with,
or my prying neighbours.

                    OLIVIA
Is it difficult keeping the
relationship under wraps at work? I
bet it's funny though.

                    ELEONORE
It's a full-time job within a full-
time job. You know, keeping the
professional demeanour when I want
to, well you know.

                    TIM
So nobody knows at the office?

                    ADAM
Everybody knows.

                    ELEONORE
What?

                    ADAM
If they didn't know, they'd ask
questions. They don't.

                    ELEONORE
Dhara has assured me none of the
girls know. It's yesterday's news
now. Have you told the boys?

                    ADAM
I haven't, but, you and I aren't the
only ones blessed with emotional
intelligence.

                    ELEONORE
Regan and Miles are definitely not
blessed, with any intelligence.

                    TIM
Eleonore, how did you do it, achieve
the impossible? Adam's actually
acquired some kind of grasp of his
emotions has he?

                    OLIVIA
          There's more to emotional
          intelligence than that darling. It's
          expressing feelings honestly, self-
          awareness, knowing how your feelings
          influence your actions, discussing
          difficult topics sensitively, active
          listening…

                    TIM
          Yeah but…

                    OLIVIA
          Including focusing on what their
          partner is saying, without
          interruption. Empathy, seeing things
          from the other's perspective, and of
          course gratitude, appreciation for
          your partner and what she does for
          you.

                    TIM
          Ads, you're way off that yet.

                    ADAM
          I believe Olivia is addressing these
          things more widely.

                    TIM
               (to Olivia)
          Darling, are you saying I'm a bit
          lacking in this area?

                    ELEONORE
          How long have you been together?

                    TIM
          Two years.

                    OLIVIA
          26 months.

Eleonore smiles at Tim.

                    ELEONORE
          Isn't it time?

                    TIM
          No, it's Tim.

                    ADAM
Oh I'm loving this. The first time my
relationship management is significantly
less important than the person next to me.

                    ELEONORE
Tim. You've got a gorgeous, caring,
funny, intelligent woman. The longest
gestation period on the planet is the
Indian Elephant, but even they're
done within a maximum of 22 months.
It's been 26 months.

                    OLIVIA
When you're ready darling. It's a
simple question with only two
possible answers. But the longer the
question takes to be asked, the more
likelihood the answer will require
thinking about. And you Eleonore,
you're awesome!

The four laugh, drink and begin a great relationship. We see
them sitting at dinner in another venue.

                    TIM
OK, what is your definition of
spontaneous?

                    OLIVIA
Grabbing an opportunity, even one you
may later regret.
     (Whispers to Tim)
Although the one I'm imagining, you
won't regret.

                    ELEONORE
Se baigner nu. (Skinny dipping)

                    TIM
     (to Adam)
Is this part of the rude vocab?

                    ELEONORE
Skinny dipping.

                    TIM
Mmm.

                    ADAM
          The Rolling Stones between 1968 and
          1972.
                    OLIVIA
          What!

                    ELEONORE
          Can't you do better than that?

                    ADAM
          There isn't any better!

                    TIM
          It was actually their best period.

                    OLIVIA
          Come on Adam, have another go.

                    ADAM
          Black raspberry chocolate chip ice
          cream. When everyone else is having
          vanilla.

                    ELEONORE
          Vanilla, yuk!

                    TIM
          We have a winner!

You're My First, The Last, My Everything by Barry White
plays.

Eleonore grabs Adam and they dance in the aisle at the
restaurant.

Olivia hugs Tim as they watch.

INT. ELEONORE'S APARTMENT - DAY

It's the next morning. Adam is waking with a hangover.
Eleonore is bringing him coffee and a pastry in bed.

She runs her hands through his dishevelled hair and smiles
lovingly.

                    ELEONORE
          She is right you know.

                    ADAM
          Good morning beautiful lady.

                    ELEONORE
          Isn't she?

                    ADAM
          Who?

                    ELEONORE
          Olivia. It is time your friend
          proposed. She clearly wants it. Women
          need certain things from their men.
          One of them being commitment.

                    ADAM
          I fancy scrambled eggs, on sourdough.
          Do you? I'll make it.

                    ELEONORE
          Yes, that would be lovely. And when
          you come back in the room, bring the
          emotionally intelligent Adam, not the
          expert at avoidance.

                    ADAM
          I don't understand. Is this about Tim
          and Olivia? It isn't, is it?

                    ELEONORE
          Do you like my apartment Adam?

                    ADAM
          Love it.

                    ELEONORE
          And you like being with me, spending
          time together, sleeping with me,
          exploring possibilities?

                    ADAM
          I do, very much, all of the above.

                    ELEONORE
          Then don't you think it's time you
          took the next step?

                    ADAM
          Marriage?

Eleonore laughs.

                    ELEONORE
          Not yet. But definitely before the
          next Indian elephant gives birth.
          Moving in. Living with your woman, in
          blissful sin.
                    ADAM
          I'd love to.

Eleonore climbs on top of Adam.

                    ELEONORE
          There are 86,400 seconds in a day.
          How many of those do you spend
          thinking about me?

                    ADAM
          Probably at least 85,000.

                    ELEONORE
          Unacceptable. That's not enough. I'm
          going to have to work on that.

INT. ELEONORE'S APARTMENT - NEXT DAY

Adam is moving his clothes and other items into the
apartment.

Eleonore is looking at what he is unpacking and laughing a
lot.

                    ELEONORE
          What is so heavy that the bag is
          splitting?

                    ADAM
          Dumbbells.

                    ELEONORE
          How often do you, dumb?

                    ADAM
          As you can see from my muscular
          frame, clearly not as often as I,
          bell. I've never used them.

                    ELEONORE
          And I guess you brought them here, to
          never use them.

                    ADAM
They're good door stops.

                    ELEONORE
And this?

                    ADAM
Buddha.

                    ELEONORE
He's very slim.

                    ADAM
Yeah, don't you think it's a tragedy
that most Buddha paraphernalia
portrays him as a lazy fat tree
dweller, rather than the true svelte
prince he was.

                    ELEONORE
I think the point is not about the
aesthetic.

                    ADAM
But he does look cool like this.

                    ELEONORE
And I'm sure that is what he would
want his lasting legacy to be.

                    ADAM
My notebooks. These are private.

                    ELEONORE
Secrets from your future wife. Not a
promising start.

                    ADAM
Darling, they're personal.

                    ELEONORE
One man's personal is another woman's
unnecessarily secret.

                    ADAM
I've had these since I was about 12.

                    ELEONORE
Can you at least tell me what you've
written about?

                    ADAM
Poems, lyrics, thoughts, dreams,
aspirations.

                    ELEONORE
That's lovely mon cœur. Perhaps
someday you will dedicate something
to me.
                    ADAM
I already have.

Adam gives Eleonore a lyric he's written called "Another Kind
Of Giving".

Eleonore takes her time to read it and is visibly touched.

                    ELEONORE
You   are   the   most   precious,
gorgeous,   sexy,   tennis   racquet
stringer I have ever met.

                    ADAM
How many have you met?

                    ELEONORE
Two.

                    ADAM
Who's the other one?

                    ELEONORE
His name is Rouge.

                    ADAM
I had a very good French teacher. And
Rouge will probably be very offended.

                    ELEONORE
I know this is awkward timing,
bearing in mind the current physical
transition, but I need to tell you,
we have visitors coming next week.

                    ADAM
Are they staying?

                    ELEONORE
Oui. For a couple of weeks.

                    ADAM
     I'd better try and keep my bathroom
     sessions down to 45 minutes then.

                    ELEONORE
     Don't you want to know who they are?

                    ADAM
     I'll take an uneducated guess and say
     they share the same surname, Garnier.
     Do they know about me?

                    ELEONORE
     Of course.

                    ADAM
     Do they know I'm moving in? How old I
     am?

                    ELEONORE
     These minor details can wait.

                    ADAM
     Well, you know them better than me
     darling.

Eleonore smiles.

                    ELEONORE
     Yes indeed. And I know if we can get
     through these two weeks, nothing will
     ever stop us being together.

Eleonore hugs and kisses Adam.

INT. ELEONORE'S APARTMENT - DAY

Mr & Mrs Garnier arrive at the apartment while Adam is at
work.

Eleonore settles them into their room and speaks to them.

                    ELEONORE
     Let's practice some English. Seems appropriate,
     bearing in mind what I have to say.

                    MRS GARNIER
     Are you frightened to say it in French?

>   ELEONORE
>   My boyfriend is staying here.
>
>   MR GARNIER
>   Depuis quand? (Since when?)
>
>   ELEONORE
>   Je suis assez vieux (I am old enough)
>
>   MRS GARNIER
>   C'était rapide. (That was quick) And the English
>   lesson is over.
>
>   MR GARNIER
>   Eleonore.

Mr Garnier is shaking his head, clearly unhappy about the situation.

INT. ELEONORE'S APARTMENT - EVENING

Adam arrives home. Eleonore quickly greets him and lets him know they've arrived.

>   ELEONORE
>   They're here.
>
>   ADAM
>   (clearly nervous)
>   Bonjour Mr and Mrs Garnier, bienvenue
>   à Londres.
>
>   MR GARNIER
>   Tu peux m'appeler Raymond, et ma
>   femme est Alice. (You can call me
>   Raymond, and my wife is Alice)
>
>   ELEONORE
>   Papa, en Anglais, s'il te plaît. (Father, please,
>   in English)
>
>   MR GARNIER
>   But Eleonore, Adam can clearly speak
>   perfect French.
>
>   MRS GARNIER
>   Raymond arrête! (Raymond stop!)
>
>   ADAM
>   I thought we'd all go out for dinner
>   tonight. Do you have a preference?

                    MR GARNIER
          Why don't you choose for us, Adam?

                    ADAM
          Yes of course.

The four go to a French restaurant. Adam is the perfect host.
Eleonore looks lovingly at him, much to the distain of her
father. Her mother seems to like Adam.

                    MR GARNIER
          I understand you make racquets for
          tennis.

                    ADAM
          Well, I don't actually make them,
          more like sabotage them.

                    MR GARNIER
          Que veux-tu dire? (What do you mean?)

                    ELEONORE
          Adam's joking papa.

                    MR GARNIER
          The British humour, yes.

Mr Garnier gets up to go to the bathroom. Mrs Garnier leans
over to Adam.

                    MRS GARNIER
          Adam, I like you. In time Raymond
          will come around, when he sees what I
          see. I know you love our daughter.
          It's the brightest beacon of light,
          more than the sun.

Eleonore is emotional. Hugs her mother.

                    ELEONORE
          Maman.

                    MRS GARNIER
          C'est un homme bon. (He's a good man)

INT. RESTAURANT - LATER (while having drinks).

                    ADAM
          Mr Garnier, do you like football?

                    MR GARNIER
          No.

                    ADAM
Do you like Music?

                    MR GARNIER
I like good music.

                    ADAM
Me too. We have that in common.

                    ELEONORE
Adam plays too. Guitar, piano. And he
writes, beautiful lyrics.

                    MR GARNIER
I'm sure Adam is talented in many
ways. A man develops certain skills
by the time he reaches the grand age
of, what is it again Adam?

                    ADAM
Mr Garnier. I love your daughter very
much. I also think this evening, as
it's your first in London since
Eleonore has moved here, should
probably be a Garnier family affair.
I should leave you all to catch up.

Eleonore bangs on the table.

                    ELEONORE
              (raised voice)
Papa, arrête ça maintenant. J'aime
Adam et il ne mérite pas ça.
(Father, stop this now. I love Adam
and he doesn't deserve this) I will
not have the man I love treated like
this. Apologise, now.

Mr Garnier does not apologise. Eleonore waits a bit longer.
When the apology is not forthcoming she kisses Adam,
passionately.

Mr Garnier gets up and leaves. Mrs Garnier smiles before
following him.

                    ELEONORE
Two good things came out of that. You
didn't reveal your age, I said you
were 21. And, we have the rest of
the wine to ourselves. Cheers.

                    ADAM
          Cheers. But what about tomorrow?

                    ELEONORE
          Don't worry about tomorrow. The
          secret weapon will be unleashed on
          Raymond tonight.

                    ADAM
          Your mother?

Eleonore raises her glass.

                    ELEONORE
          Oui. To Alice.

Adam raises his glass.

                    ADAM
          To Alice.

INT. ELEONORE'S APARTMENT - DAY

The following day Eleonore is up early and getting ready to
take her mother shopping in London.

                    ADAM
          What time is it?

                    ELEONORE
          7:00. You need to get up. There is a
          queue of future Wimbledon Champions
          waiting for you to provide your very
          magic touch to their racquets.

                    ADAM
          Are you not working today?

                    ELEONORE
          I'm taking maman to Knightsbridge.

                    ADAM
          What about Raymond?

                    ELEONORE
          My mother told him he must stay home,
          until he learns how to behave; watch
          English TV.

                    ADAM
          Goodness! That's a bit harsh. We
          usually reserve that punishment for
          career criminals and politicians.
          Please be home before me.

                    ELEONORE
          We will. I love you.

                    ADAM
          You're not too bad yourself.

INT. SPORTS WAREHOUSE - DAY

Lunchtime at the sports warehouse. Red comes in to speak to
Adam.

                    RED
          Do you know a strange man with a
          strange accent and a strange hat.

                    ADAM
          I don't think so.

                    RED
          Well, he knows you, at least your
          name. He said, he's come to meet you
          for lunch. He's in Reception.

Adam looks at the CCTV. He sees Mr Garnier.

                    ADAM
          Oh God.

                    RED
          Who is he?

                    ADAM
          He's…a family friend.

                    RED
          Your family?

                    ADAM
          The Adams Family. Can I take an early
          lunch.

                    RED
          Go on. Say hello to Lurch for me. Or
          should I say Monsieur Lurch?

                    ADAM
          You know, don't you?

                    RED
          What do I know? That you have never
          spoken to Eleonore since Jade's
          leaving party. That you distance
          yourself from the lads outside
          lately. That she always sends Dhara
          down here now. That you arrive at
          work pretty much the same time as her
          every day.
          And now, when her parents are coming
          to visit, a serious looking man with
          a French accent comes to take you to
          lunch. Advantage Red.

                    ADAM
          You're the man!

EXT. MEETING LOCATION - DAY

Adam goes to meet Mr Garnier.

                    ADAM
          Bonjour Raymond.

                    MR GARNIER
          Bonjour. Time for a little lunch?

                    ADAM
          I've only got an hour, but yes,
          great. Is there anything you'd like
          in particular.

                    MR GARNIER
          It's not about the food, more the
          company.

                    ADAM
          That's a little un-French, isn't it?

Mr Garnier half-smiles, but is not warm to Adam.

INT. CAFE - DAY

A local café. Mr Garnier is drinking coffee. Adam has tea and
is waiting for his food.

                    ADAM
Are you sure you won't eat? I feel
bad eating if you're not.

                    MR GARNIER
My appetite is not so good. Maybe too
much rich food last night.

                    ADAM
I hope Mrs Garnier and Eleonore are
having a successful shopping
expedition.

                    MR GARNIER
I'm sure they are. They are very
close. We all are. A very close
family. I had hoped in time, Eleonore
would meet a man to be her husband
and make us four again. You know we
lost a son, many years ago.

                    ADAM
Yes, I'm really sorry.

                    MR GARNIER
Unfortunately, these things happen.
C'est la vie. But we are very
grateful to have such a wonderful,
beautiful daughter.

                    ADAM
She's amazing.

                    MR GARNIER
Adam, perhaps I was a little harsh
last night.

                    ADAM
It's OK.

                    MR GARNIER
I am a protective father, for sure.

                    ADAM
That's understandable.

                    MR GARNIER
          I'm glad you understand. There is
          something else you need to
          understand. You and Eleonore, it's
          not real. I'm sure you might have
          some kind of fantasy about a
          beautiful French woman; someone who
          is destined for greater things, as
          she is, and the attention she is
          currently giving you. But it's not
          lasting. Surely you can see that. A
          woman like our daughter; she can do
          much better. It's possible you love
          her, or think you do. But if you love
          her, really care for her, value her,
          want a great future for her, as her
          mother and I do, you will do the only
          decent thing you can do, break off
          the relationship. Find someone, more
          your own level, be happy, you deserve
          happiness, so does Eleonore.

                    ADAM
          Is this your first visit to London?

                    MR GARNIER
          I came once as a child.

                    ADAM
          I've never been to Paris. So it's
          safe to say we've never met. All you
          can know about me, is what Eleonore's
          told you, and I have a very strong
          feeling that's all positive. So, the
          assessment you've made of me, is
          understandably grossly inaccurate.

                    MR GARNIER
          Eleonore loves her family. She will
          not want to bring a man into it who
          does not have the family's blessing.
          Adam, you know in your heart, she can
          do better. Do the right thing, for
          Eleonore.

Mr Garnier gets up to leave as Adam's food arrives. The
waiter speaks to Adam.

                    WAITER
          Isn't he staying?

                    ADAM
          No. He always leaves before paying. I
          think he's French royalty. What I
          wouldn't give for a guillotine right
          now.

INT. SPORTS WAREHOUSE - DAY

Adam comes back to work. Red can see he's upset.

                    RED
          Not a good lunch?

                    ADAM
          Who's the best tennis player you've
          ever seen play?

                    RED
          Sampras, at his peak.

                    ADAM
          The worst?

                    RED
          My P.E. teacher.

                    ADAM
          Imagine a match between them. It
          wouldn't last long, it would be
          completely one-sided, and as far as
          the entertainment value…

                    RED
          He's not Sampras, and while I haven't
          seen you play, I am very sure you
          would kick my old P.E. teacher's ass
          all around the court.

                    ADAM
          Thank you, but I feel it was game,
          set and match, to Raymond Sampras.

                    RED
          Then go and practice. Kick the crap
          out of him next time.

Adam smiles and goes back to work.

INT. ELEONORE'S APARTMENT - DAY

Over the next two weeks the atmosphere it home is polite,
with Adam being particularly friendly to Mrs Garnier. When
they leave for Paris Adam is conveniently busy.

EXT. LOCAL PARK - DAY

The local park. Adam and Tim are playing football 1 versus 1.
Adam is easily better than Tim.

                    TIM
          The man is a complete bastard.

                    ADAM
          Understatement Timothy. 6-1.

                    TIM
          Are you going to tell Eleonore?

                    ADAM
          How can I?

                    TIM
          He's out of the way now. Forget about
          him.

                    ADAM
          I don't know Tim. There's probably a
          lot in what he says.

                    TIM
          Didn't your grandmother have a
          saying?

                    ADAM
          There's no such word as can't.

                    TIM
          Exactly. So he's full of crap. Right?

                    ADAM
          Yes, as crap as you are at
          football. 7-1!

INT. ELEONORE'S APARTMENT - DAY

It's now a couple of months later and Adam is being
spontaneous. Eleonore arrives home from work; Adam is in the
apartment.

                    ADAM
          Surprise Eleonore!

                    ELEONORE
          Wow! No one has ever bought me
          swimwear, apart from my mother. And
          it was sufficiently smaller as I
          remember, and a little less sexy.

Shall I try it on now?

                    ADAM
Yes please. You're gonna look
gorgeous in the Greek sunshine.

                    ELEONORE
Greece!

                    ADAM
I'm taking you island hopping, I'm
going to hire a motorbike, we're
gonna have so much fun. Copious
amount of alcohol and lots of bad
behaviour.

                    ELEONORE
You're full of surprises lately Adam.
What next, a marriage proposal?

                    ADAM
You and me, out there, deserted
beaches, music, starry nights, who
knows what might happen.

                    ELEONORE
Can't wait.

INT. CENTRAL LONDON CAFE - DAY

Eleonore is having a late lunch in central London with
Olivia. She's just been for an interview for a great job
nearby.

                    ELEONORE
It seemed they were asking the
perfect questions. I could have
written them. And the CEO, Greg,
Australian, he could be a great
mentor.

                    OLIVIA
How exciting! Do they know at work?

                    ELEONORE
No, I'll tell them if I get the job.
Olivia this job will be perfect for
me, and for Adam too.

                    OLIVIA
What, you mean not working together,
yeah I can see that will be majorly

beneficial, now you're living
together. Shameful, by the way.

                    ELEONORE
Olivia, how well do you know Adam?

                    OLIVIA
I met him through Tim, and I think he
has two distinct sides to his
character, but I'm very sure you know
that and much more about him than I
do. Maybe even more than Tim.

                    ELEONORE
What are the two sides?

                    OLIVIA
The confident and the insecure.

                    ELEONORE
Tell me.

                    OLIVIA
He's lovely Eleonore. But pretty much
until he met you his confidence was
just a show. He'd play upon the
charm, the good looks, the humour,
but Tim's told me a few other things
and I've seen some of the not so
self-assured. I don't even think he
would have ever asked you out if he
didn't rely on Southern Comfort or
the house of Guinness to push him.

                    ELEONORE
I know.

                    OLIVIA
Tim told me something Adam said after
your first weekend.

                    ELEONORE
What?

                    OLIVIA
I shouldn't. Promise you won't repeat
this.
                    ELEONORE
Promise.

                    OLIVIA
He said he'd met this amazing woman,
and she seemed to be into him, but

that it could never be permanent,
because she was much too good for him
and couldn't possibly want him long-
term. He was torn between getting out
then or seeing how long you would let
the relationship run.

                    ELEONORE
God. Adam!

                    OLIVIA
He seems a lot more confident now
though. You're obviously really good
for him. How do you feel?

                    ELEONORE
We're good for each other. I try to
reassure him, about my intentions,
and it seems everything is
understood, and then he'll do or say
something that, you know,
contradicts.

                    OLIVIA
But you're going to the Greek islands
soon, perhaps that will be the moment
of realisation. The future defining
trip.

                    ELEONORE
I really think so.

INT. ELEONORE'S APARTMENT - ONE WEEK LATER

Eleonore is on the sofa watching a film and looking a little
bit down.

                    ADAM
Is it that job? I know how much you
wanted it. What kind of idiots
wouldn't appoint the most talented,
and let's face it, sexiest Finance
manager in London?

                    ELEONORE
I love you.

                    ADAM
Je t'aime aussi.

INT. OFFICE - DAY

The next day Eleonore is in the office and asks Dhara to cover a meeting while she takes a call. The call is international.

                    KATIE
          Can I speak with Eleonore please?

                    ELEONORE
          Eleonore speaking.

                    KATIE
          Hi, it's Katie, Mr Simon's P.A. He's
          in Sydney at the moment but has asked
          me to arrange an urgent conference
          call. I know it's short notice but he
          has a packed diary at the moment. Is
          there any way possible you could do
          6pm your time today?

                    ELEONORE
          Yes of course.

                    KATIE
          Excellent. Expect a call from him at
          6. Thanks so much Eleonore, have a
          lovely day!

Adam isn't at work today; he's shopping for clothes and making final arrangements for the Greece trip.

Eleonore calls him but he's on the phone booking a motorbike.

                    ADAM (V.O.)
          It doesn't have to be fast, just
          reliable, and pretty of course.
          Actually, the opposite of the ones we
          used to acquire when I was younger.
          Don't worry, nothing. Do I pay now?

                    ELEONORE
          Adam. Adam pick up!

Adam's phone goes to voicemail.

                    ELEONORE
          Mon coeur, the CEO from the company

          who interviewed me last month wants
          to call at 6pm, from Sydney! And I
          know we're going out but I'll meet

you about half hour later, maybe with
some great news!

INT. GREG'S HOUSE - NIGHT

Greg is arriving home to his beach side house after a late-
night party. Just before going to bed he calls Eleonore.

                    GREG
          Hello Eleonore, Greg Simon, how are
          you today?

                    ELEONORE
          Hello Greg. I'm great thanks.
          Surprised to hear from your company,
          and from you.

                    GREG
          Yes, sorry we had to delay making our
          decision, there have been a few
          things going on behind the scenes.

                    ELEONORE
          Sounds interesting.

                    GREG
          I'll get to the point because I
          imagine you have other plans on a
          Friday evening. We're expanding,
          which is why I'm in Sydney at the
          moment.

                    ELEONORE
          Fantastic!

                    GREG
          Yes indeed, a fantastic opportunity
          for us and as I'm sure you'd agree
          sometimes you have to grab
          opportunities when they come up, even
          if the timing isn't perfect.

                    ELEONORE
          Yes of course.

                    GREG
          I want you to lead our Finance Team
          at the Sydney office. I know you
          might think it's a bit of a leap from
          your current position but we were so
          impressed with you, your attitude and
          your obvious ability; you are
          definitely the right person to manage

our new team. It's a very exciting
time. The package will include
relocation and some other benefits
that I can get Katie to email you
details of, assuming you're still
interested.

                    ELEONORE
This is, surprising. I don't know
what to say.

                    GREG
Obviously the word I'd like to
hear has three letters. Yes, or
Oui, are both acceptable.

                    ELEONORE
Can I talk about it with my partner?

                    GREG
Yes please do. But if I could ask
that you get back to Katie first
thing on Monday morning. It's all
happening very quickly over here
right now.

                    ELEONORE
Yes, I'll do that. Thank you so much.
Have a lovely evening, oh morning
isn't it.

                    GREG
It is here. Time isn't the only
difference Eleonore. I think you're
going to find lots of positive life
changes if you grab this opportunity.

                    ELEONORE
Thank you. Goodbye Greg.

INT. BAR - EVENING

Adam's in a bar with a drink ready for Eleonore. He wants to
give her some news, and hopes after her recent call it will
be a double celebration.

                    ADAM
     Hey.

Adam kisses her.

                    ADAM
Looking gorgeous as ever. I've got
the details about our trip and…do you
remember me telling you about my
aunt, the only one not from the poor
side of the family. She's got the
place in Notting Hill, well
Kensington really. That beautiful
grand apartment with the balcony
coming out onto the square. She wants
us to look after it for at least a
year while she's away. You can rent
out your place. Half the people in
the square are either famous actors
or rock stars!

                    ELEONORE
I have some news too. I've been
offered that job.

                    ADAM
Fantastic! That's in Central London
as well.

                    ELEONORE
No.

                    ADAM
No?

                    ELEONORE
Not Central London. Sydney, Australia.

                    ADAM
Wow. Too far to commute.

                    ELEONORE
Adam, I want us to discuss it.

                    ADAM
Eleonore...

                    ELEONORE
I didn't know they were opening in
Australia; nothing was mentioned in
the interview. The CEO called. I'm
not sure I'll ever have an
opportunity like this again. Mon
coeur I want to go and I want you to
come with me. I want to make a
commitment to you.

FLASHBACK - INT/ADAMS CHILDHOOD HOME -

Adam flashes back to being 6 years old. A narrow hallway, his father at one end looking upset, his mother at the end with a suitcase about to leave. His father asking if he wants to stay, his mother asking if he wants to come with her. Adam is still.

END OF FLASHBACK.

                    ADAM
          You should go. It's what you want.

                    ELEONORE
          And you. You'll come?

                    ADAM
          I don't think so.

                    ELEONORE
          Why?

                    ADAM
          You said it yourself. This is an
          amazing opportunity for you. Having
          me there you wouldn't be focused on
          making it the success that I know you
          can, I know you will. Look, we can
          see how it goes for a few months
          and...

                    ELEONORE
              (becoming angry)
          And what? Then see how it goes for
          another few months? And then the
          messages and phone calls become
          gradually less, and then one of us,
          or both of us, are socialising and
          out of touch for a couple of days the
          other one starts to imagine what is
          happening, or worse still doesn't
          imagine anything because they no
          longer care enough to worry about it!

                    ADAM
          I didn't know your talents, of which
          there are many, included seeing the
          future.

                    ELEONORE
          I want to see the future with you
          Adam. I've wanted that since I first
          saw you struggling to tie a knot in

that tennis racquet with those...
pince métallique.

                    ADAM
Needle nose pliers.

                    ELEONORE
Yes, needle nose pliers.

                    ADAM
Sounds sexy when you say it, French
girl.

                    ELEONORE
If we're over ten thousand miles
apart how can we?

                    ADAM
It looks like we're about to find
out. Please promise me one thing.

                    ELEONORE
What?

                    ADAM
If you meet someone in a bar, you
won't dance to Staying Alive and then
later on have it as your song at your
wedding reception.

                    ELEONORE
That wasn't the song that was playing
when I pulled you onto the dance
floor.

                    ADAM
What song was playing?

                    ELEONORE
It was Brown Sugar. The Rolling
Stones.

                    ADAM
From 1971, in their best period.

                    ELEONORE
So I've been told. When they were
particularly, what's the word,
spontaneous.

                    ADAM
Like you are now.

                    ELEONORE
Like you clearly don't want to be.

                    ADAM
It's not…

                    ELEONORE
And you Adam, when will be your best
period?

                    ADAM
When I meet the woman I love…

                    ELEONORE
I thought you already had…

                    ADAM
Again.

INT. COFFEE BAR - AIRPORT - DAY

Eleonore, Dhara and Olivia are in a coffee bar at the
airport.

                    DHARA
I'm so proud of you. You know how
much I love you. How could you do
this to me?

                    ELEONORE
You got a new job, mine!

                    DHARA
I'd rather have you here.

                    OLIVIA
How are you? You know.

                    ELEONORE
A combination of heartbreak,
trepidation and excitement.

                    OLIVIA
In that order?

                    ELEONORE
Oui.

                    DHARA
She only speaks French when she's
emotional, or swearing at management
under her breath.

                    ELEONORE
          That first night, with Adam. I
          thought I had him wrapped around my
          finger.

                    DHARA
          You most certainly did.

                    ELEONORE
          Then why isn't he here now?

                    OLIVIA
          He'll come round. In less than a
          couple of weeks he'll be turning up
          unannounced, telling you how much he
          misses you and can't live without
          you. And if he doesn't, I'll send Tim
          to go and live with him until he's
          desperate to leave. A couple of
          nights of being exposed to Tim's
          snoring should do it.

                    ELEONORE
          Thanks, you are both…I love you. And
          whatever happens, next Christmas,
          it's girls' night out at Bondi beach,
          deal?

                    OLIVIA / DHARA
          Deal!

EXT/INT. ADAM'S NEW HOME - WEST LONDON - DAY

Adam is moving some things into his new temporary home in
West London. He's living in a beautiful square but his head
is going round in circles. His bravado, evident since
meeting Eleonore, has given way to an unrelenting and very
familiar insecurity.

On the mantel are two tickets to Greece and a motor bike
rental agreement.

He pours a Southern Comfort Black and steps out onto the
balcony. Music is playing. This time it really is The Bee
Gees. He's daydreaming about Eleonore and the beautiful and
poignant "Words" plays in the background. Someone appears on
the adjacent balcony. She looks friendly and bohemian,
wearing an unmatching multi coloured skirt, tunic and head
scarf ensemble. She smiles at Adam and speaks to him.

                    GRACE
          Hello. That's retro.

                    ADAM
          Sorry it's probably louder than it
          should be. I'm new to the
          neighbourhood. I imagine excessively
          loud pre-Night Fever Bee Gees
          contravenes the local rules and regs.

                    GRACE
          The resident's association might
          object but I'm not a lover of rules.
          Are you?

                    ADAM
          That is an interesting question. If
          I'm in the midst of a game I would
          like to know if there are rules.
          Because if only one player thinks
          there are and the other doesn't, it
          wouldn't be fair. Don't you think?

                    GRACE
          My name's Grace.

                    ADAM
          Mine's Adam.

                    GRACE
          Well Adam, from this balcony, I'd say
          it's a lot more healthy to skip the
          games altogether. La vida es corta,
          as the Spanish say.

                    ADAM
          Would you like to come to this
          balcony and have a drink, Grace?
          That's a lovely name.

Adam opens the front door. Grace doesn't come in.

                    ADAM
          It's open.

                    GRACE
          I know but I need an invite. I'm a
          vampire.

                    ADAM
          Thank God. I need protection from the
          resident's association. I hear
          they're after me for playing pre-
          Night Fever Bee Gees, loudly. Anyway,
          please come in.

                    GRACE
          Thank you. I'm sure we'll find a way
          to keep them at bay. Southern
          Comfort, the hard stuff.

                    ADAM
          Actually, Southern Comfort Black.

                    GRACE
          What's the difference?

                    ADAM
          The original is 35% alcohol, Black is
          40.

                    GRACE
          And is that 5% important?

                    ADAM
          Probably not, but the bottle's
          prettier.

                    GRACE
          And pretty is important to Adam I'm
          guessing.

                    ADAM
          What can I get you Grace?

                    GRACE
          I don't suppose you've got some white
          tea; nobody does.

                    ADAM
          Tea with milk?

                    GRACE
          No. It's like green tea, but the buds
          are younger, it's more pure, has lots
          of antioxidants, neutralizes free
          radicals. Lots of health benefits.

Adam thinks of Eleonore, speaking French in the bar on their
first night.

                    ADAM
          You must know I didn't understand a
          word of that. Feels like déjà vu.

                    GRACE
          Good déjà vu?

                    ADAM
          Yes, very good déjà vu.

We see Adam over the next few days periodically looking out
of the open balcony door clearly hoping to see his new
neighbour again.

Finally, Grace reappears.

                    GRACE
          Hey Adam.

                    ADAM
          Grace. How are you? Thought you'd
          gone away.

                    GRACE
          Not going away anytime soon I'm
          afraid.

                    ADAM
          If you could go somewhere, where
          would you go?

                    GRACE
          I don't know maybe somewhere like
          Greece?

                    ADAM
          Really!

                    GRACE
          I'm messing with you Adam. I saw the
          tickets when you were making me tea.

                    ADAM
          Yeah sorry about that, I know you
          wanted that special tea. I'm going to
          get some. Need to go on a health
          kick, like yesterday.

                    GRACE
          It's fine. When are you off to the
          sun?

                    ADAM
          On Saturday.

                    GRACE
          Are you going with friends? A
          significant other?

                    ADAM
          That was the plan. I think I'm going
          alone now.

                    GRACE
          It looks that way if you're leaving
          in two days. I mean who are you going
          to find that's available at short
          notice, hasn't got any current
          commitments and lives close enough to
          share a taxi to the airport without
          it needing to make an unnecessary
          stop?

                    ADAM
          Are you saying what I think you're
          saying?

                    GRACE
          Yes I'd love to come Adam. Thanks for
          the invite!

                    ADAM
          Oh my goodness. I'm going to Grace,
          with Greece!

                    GRACE
          That's the wrong way round.

                    ADAM
          Yeah I know. OK, to save confusion
          have you got a middle name?

                    GRACE
          Eve.

                    ADAM
          You're not serious!

                    GRACE
          I'm rarely serious. You'll get to
          know that, and potentially despair of
          it.

                    ADAM
          This is going to be so much fun!

                    GRACE
          I hope so.

Adam is on the phone to Tim.

                    ADAM
             (into phone)
     Guess what?

                    TIM (V.O.)
     This could take a while. A while with
     anyone, but with you several
     lifetimes.

                    ADAM
     My neighbour is coming to Greece with
     me.

                    TIM (V.O.)
     The weird girl next door?

                    ADAM
     Mate she's lovely.

                    TIM (V.O.)
     What are you going to tell Eleonore?

                    ADAM
     Please don't mention it to Olivia.
     Not yet.

                    TIM (V.O.)
     Ads, are you sure this is a good idea?

                    ADAM
     Grace is just a friend.

                    TIM (V.O.)
     It does make you wonder though. Why
     is she going with you?

                    ADAM
     Thanks!

                    TIM (V.O.)
     No seriously, you hardly know each
     other. What's the deal with her?

                    ADAM
     I don't know, maybe she's spontaneous.

                    TIM (V.O.)
     Yeah, you've experienced that
     recently, how did it end again?
     Listen mate, don't do anything that
     you'll regret. Don't do anything you
     can't undo.

                    ADAM
          I won't.

INT. GRACE'S APARTMENT - DAY

Grace is asking her neighbour, Vincenzo, to help get her
suitcase down from on top of the wardrobe.

We see crutches in the vicinity and Grace occasionally
breathes slightly heavily.

Vincenzo looks at her affectionately.

                    GRACE
          Thanks so much Vincenzo, you are a
          star, as ever.

                    VINCENZO
          Are you sure about this?

                    GRACE
          What is there to be sure about? The
          only thing that's definite is the
          non- infinite existence, and the only
          thing that's essential is to do more
          of whatever brings us joy, to take
          opportunities, chances, while we can.

                    VINCENZO
          He's only just moved here; we don't
          know anything about him. You don't
          know anything about him.

                    GRACE
          I do.

                    VINCENZO
          What?

                    GRACE
          I imagine he's recently broken up
          with his girlfriend, who was probably
          going with him, and now he's very
          probably thinking about finding
          himself, on a deserted beach
          somewhere. And probably needs a
          friend, some guidance.

                    VINCENZO
          There's a lot of probably's in the
          air today Grace.

                    GRACE
          Possibly. Anyway, thank you. You're
          the best. Now go back to your wife
          and enjoy that lovely Italian food. I
          can smell it from here.

                    VINCENZO
          Will you join us?

                    GRACE
          I need a rest. But if you ask me
          tomorrow, I'll eat you out of house
          and home!

EXT. NEIGHBORHOOD - DAY

Saturday comes and the neighbours leave for the airport in a
taxi.

                    GRACE
          You   might   be   thinking,   this
          whole situation is odd. If you
          are, try looking at it through a
          different perspective.

                    ADAM
          I'm up for that.

                    GRACE
          What is life made of?

                    ADAM
          I was never any good at science.

                    GRACE
          Me neither. But I imagine you're
          quite a perceptive person.

                    ADAM
          I have been accused, some say
          falsely, of having a good level of
          emotional intelligence.

                    GRACE
          A great place to start.

                    ADAM
          Go on.

                    GRACE
If we accept life happens to us, if
we accept fate, inevitability, then
we surrender control, which in other
circumstances would be seen as a very
clumsy strategy. For example,
trusting a child with something that
could be dangerous.

                    ADAM
Yes.

                    GRACE
You wouldn't would you?

                    ADAM
I wouldn't.

                    GRACE
All that we've learned, about
percentages, taking the safer option,
weighing up risk, these things are
not in sync with what life is really
made of. Moments. Adam, life, the joy
of life, is made of moments. Those
special times that some people never
get to experience, others maybe just
experience very few, but if you're
lucky, truly blessed, you might just
have enough of those moments to warm
the coldest nights, and when you're
looking back on your life, those
moments will allow you the most
beautiful inner smile. Isn't that way
better than being safe and very
probably having regrets about what
you didn't do?

                    ADAM
Grace, you are a one-off aren't you?

                    GRACE
Maybe.

                    ADAM
When I booked this trip I had a
different kind of adventure in mind,
but I'm already starting to realise,
well, I don't know exactly what I'm
realising, but I'm really glad you
came.

                    GRACE
          Thanks, retro man.

                    ADAM
          Me! Oh, the music. What about you,
          retro woman, what's with the clothes,
          and just how many of those head
          scarfs have you packed?

                    GRACE
          It's been a bad hair month. I
          sometimes need a confidence boost.

                    ADAM
          I think we have a lot in common.

INT. ELEONORE'S OFFICE - SYDNEY - DAY

Eleonore is finding the transition more difficult than she
thought it would be. The job is really challenging. Dhara
calls to see how it's going.

                    DHARA
          Bonjour. What the hell time is it
          there?

                    ELEONORE
          You have no idea how good it is to
          hear your voice.

                    DHARA
          We're all missing you! Miles and
          Regan are running wild without you to
          sort them out, and I'm still amazed
          no one has realised how much I'm
          faking, just about everything. I bet
          you're in control though.

                    ELEONORE
          The job is stretching me a little.
          The thing that drives me is Greg's
          faith in my ability and not wanting
          to let him down. Sometimes though. At
          least when I was in London I had
          friends close by, family just across
          La Manche, and I had him. Have you
          seen him?

                    DHARA
          He's taken leave this week.

                    ELEONORE
We've been exchanging messages, not
yet spoken. I'm going to call late
tomorrow, when he's probably
listening to music and chilling. We
have things we need to say. I
certainly do.

                    DHARA
Eleonore, there's something else
isn't there?

                    ELEONORE
Let me just make sure no one's in
earshot. Greg's brother is a silent
partner and the brother's wife is a
Director, Teagan. She's my manager.
And she's taken an instant dislike to
me.

                    DHARA
Are you sure? New job, new life, new
hemisphere, could you be being a
little over sensitive?

                    ELEONORE
Ok a bit of detail. Our first
meeting. Several other people were
there, she was fine. They all left
and she asked me to stay behind. She
then told me I was probably only
appointed because her brother-in-law
had non-professional ideas and
desires, and that I am clearly in a
role that is way above my ability.
Oh, and if I ever meet her husband
I'm to make my excuses and leave.
Over sensitive?

                    DHARA
What a bitch! Jealous cow. I wanna
slap her.

                    ELEONORE
Thanks dear. I have one positive in
the whole situation. He's very
supportive and not the least bit
intimidated by her. His name's Paul,
we're having a drink after work. He's
a senior manager, definitely knows
his stuff.

                    DHARA
Mmm, Paul! How old is he?

                    ELEONORE
Mid, late 30s I think.

                    DHARA
Married? Girlfriend? Boyfriend?

                    ELEONORE
I don't know and anyway I'm not
looking, you know that. I still have
hope.

                    DHARA
Well, the man holding your hopes
needs to get his ass over to Sydney
soon.
He's the one who should be supporting
you.

                    ELEONORE
We'll resolve it, we always do. Get
back to work now. Show them you're
better than the last manager.

                    DHARA
Call me, I miss you!

                    ELEONORE
Bye dear.

Eleonore goes to the kitchen to make a coffee and is
approached by Teagan.

                    TEAGAN
Busy?

                    ELEONORE
I think so, yes. How are you?

                    TEAGAN
Make sure the Operational Review
Report is done by the close of play
tomorrow. I don't like tardy.

                    ELEONORE
I'll try. It's a big piece of work. I'll
work late tonight and tomorrow, hopefully
it…

                    TEAGAN
          There's no way hopefully is going to
          be anywhere good enough.

                    ELEONORE
          Of course. It will be on your desk by
          close of play tomorrow.

                    TEAGAN
          Good. I'm glad we understand each
          other.

Teagan leaves. Eleonore anxiously checks her phone.

EXT. OFFICE - DAY

We see Eleonore leaving the office.

INT. RESTAURANT - CONTINUOUS

Eleonore heads to a restaurant, where Paul is waiting. He is
well dressed, confident and polite.

                    PAUL
          Hey newbie!

                    ELEONORE
          Hello.

                    PAUL
          Before you say anything, let me tell
          you what is not going to happen
          tonight. I'm not going to take you
          home, although I will make sure you
          get home safely. I'm not going to
          tell you, your Director is going to
          soften, although I will arm you with
          a few techniques to stop the
          attempted Tasman Tsunami she's famous
          for whipping up. I'm not going to ask
          you any searching personal questions,
          apart from are you vegan, you're not
          are you?

Eleonore smiles.

                    ELEONORE
          No, I'm French.

                    PAUL
          Great! And lastly, feel free to vent,
          in French, English or any other
          language or dialect that comes to
          mind. And be prepared to be taught a
          few choice Sydney ways to curse. We
          all need each other round here.

Eleonore is looking reassured and comfortable with Paul.

EXT. NAXOS - DAY

Adam and Grace are riding around the Greek island of Naxos on
his rented motorbike. We see them stop at a café bar
overlooking the Aegean Sea.

Grace looks out dreamily at the view.

                    GRACE
          So beautiful. Thanks Adam.

                    ADAM
          No way. Thank you Grace. We were
          meant to meet, don't you think?

                    GRACE
          Oh, come off it, cut the fate crap.
          It was just your dodgy taste in music
          that got me onto the balcony. No fate
          in that. More like curious annoyance.

                    ADAM (smiling)
          You're amazing.

FLASHBACK - PHONECALL'S LOCATION - NIGHT

ADAM CONCURRENTLY HAS A FLASHBACK TO SAYING THOSE WORDS TO
ELEONORE ON THEIR PHONE CALL AFTER THE FIRST WEEKEND
TOGETHER.

END OF FLASHBACK.

                    ADAM
          Amazing Grace. Saved a wretch like me.

                    GRACE
          Sinful and unworthy are you? Well that's
          one for God, not Grace.

Grace caringly takes Adam's hand.

                    GRACE
          It will work out. Whatever it is.
          Some people are very clearly meant to
          make it. And you, dodgy bike rider,
          retro boy, are definitely one of
          them.

Adam smiles again and they both look out at the sea.

INT. ADAM'S HOTEL ROOM - NIGHT

It's late at night and Grace is sleeping in the adjoining
room to Adam. Adam is sitting on the ledge looking out at
the night and listening to the waves. He gets a call.

                    ELEONORE (V.O.)
          Adam.

                    ADAM
          Hello beautiful.

                    ELEONORE (V.O.)
          I wanted to call earlier today but
          thought I'd try and catch you before
          you go to bed. It's 10am tomorrow
          here.

                    ADAM
          It's just gone 1am here.

                    ELEONORE (V.O.)
          Oh, sorry I thought you were 11 hours
          behind.

                    ADAM
          Not in Naxos.

                    ELEONORE (V.O.)
          Oh of course. You went, well that's
          fantastic! Are you having fun?

                    ADAM
          Yes, but I'm missing you a lot.

                    ELEONORE (V.O.)
          Come here then. You won't need any
          more than your fare and I'm sure Red
          will let you, just for a while. I can
          speak with him if you like.

                    ADAM
I don't work there anymore. I haven't
told them yet but I'm not going back.

                    ELEONORE (V.O.)
What happened?

                    ADAM
You happened. After that everything
went a bit crazy, beautiful crazy.

                    ELEONORE (V.O.)
So you just went to Greece on your
own?

                    ADAM
No. I came with a friend, a
neighbour. She's going back on
Saturday. I'm staying out here a bit
longer.

                    ELEONORE (V.O.)
She?

                    ADAM
Her name's Grace. She's just a
friend, could obviously never be
anything more.

                    ELEONORE (V.O.)
It all sounds a bit, odd.

                    ADAM
I'm wondering if it matters that much
anyway. Don't you think that no
matter what feelings you may have for
another person, sometimes they may be
on a different path and...

                    ELEONORE (V.O.)
Stop it Adam! Ask me why I'm calling.

                    ADAM
Why are you calling Eleonore?

                    ELEONORE (V.O.)
To ask you one more time, to come and
be with me. Come and make a future
with me.

                    ADAM
          This happened so fast; I thought we
          would carry on seeing each other,
          having fun, then being together here
          on the islands, and in a moment you
          were in Sydney and I wonder if I was
          there, you might eventually have the
          realisation that maybe I'm not the
          one you want long term.

                    ELEONORE (V.O.)
          Perhaps you could think enough of me
          to value my opinion on that?

                    ADAM
          I do. I value everything you say and
          everything you do. I think about you
          all the time. And I really want you
          to make a success of your life.

                    ELEONORE (V.O.)
          Adam, answer one question. Do you
          love me?

                    ADAM
          Yes. Of course I love you, how could
          I not?

                    ELEONORE (V.O.)
          What else matters then?... Oh God,
          Adam, I have to go, I'm being called
          into a meeting. Let's speak later. I
          love you.

                    ADAM
               (to himself)
          I love you too Eleonore and j'ai tant
          besoin de toi.(I need you so much)

INT. GRACE'S HOTEL ROOM - NIGHT

We see Grace awake in the next room.

                    GRACE
               (to herself)
          You'll be fine, retro boy.

INT. ADAM'S HOTEL - DAY

Adam has practically no sleep following the call and now
spends a final day with Grace. They are seen laughing and
very happy.

INT/EXT. HOTEL - DAY

Grace leaves a note for Adam to see when he wakes: "Hope you enjoy the rest of your adventure, my wayward boy. Please have twice the amount of fun so I can enjoy it vicariously. Bring me something back from Ios, or wherever else you may end up. And bring the sun too. Looking forward to seeing you in a couple of weeks. Love Grace. XX"

We see Grace get in a cab to the airport while Adam is still sleeping.

INT. HOTEL - DAY

Adam wakes and reads the note. He lovingly folds it and puts it in his bag.

EXT. FERRY PORT - DAY

Adam is now heading to the next island. While he's waiting for the ferry, he calls Tim.

                    ADAM
               (into phone)
          Tim.

                    TIM (V.O.)
          Hey Ads. Where are you?

                    ADAM
          Hey mate. Just leaving Naxos and
          going to Ios.

                    TIM (V.O.)
          Is your woman with you?

                    ADAM
          If you mean Grace, the neighbour who
          is not my woman, she's gone home. She
          was only ever going to stay two
          weeks. Actually, she was really tired
          the second week.

                    TIM (V.O.)
          Did anything happen?

                    ADAM
          No! She just wanted to come for
          the trip. You have to meet her;
          she's a wonderful, lovely person.

                    TIM (V.O.)
But she's not Eleonore.

                    ADAM
No one is.

                    TIM (V.O.)
Except, Eleonore. The woman you
should be with.

                    ADAM
I know. She called the other night
from Australia.

                    TIM (V.O.)
And?

                    ADAM
She asked me to go. I didn't say yes.
A big part of me knows that was a
mistake.

                    TIM (V.O.)
Then correct it. Get over there!

                    ADAM
I'm here for a little while longer.
It'll give me time to think.

                    TIM (V.O.)
At least she doesn't know you went to
Greece with a woman does she.

                    ADAM
Erm.

                    TIM (V.O.)
You didn't tell her!

                    ADAM
I just told her the truth that Grace
is my neighbour and there's nothing
in it.

                    TIM (V.O.)
And you honestly expect she's gonna
believe that!

                    ADAM
It's the truth!

                    TIM (V.O.)
          Since when did the truth matter?
          You've told the woman you love, who
          you didn't go to Australia with, that
          you've been riding around the Greek
          Islands with your new posh Notting
          Hill neighbour, while she's on her
          own in Sydney, a city of over 5
          million people with a very good
          chance one or more of those will be
          happy to console her.

                    ADAM
          We didn't finish. She had to go to a
          meeting. We'll probably speak again
          in the next couple of days,
          hopefully.

                    TIM (V.O.)
          Man, Eleonore is more than awesome.

                    ADAM
          I know. Gotta get my bike; we're
          boarding the ferry. Speak later yeah?

EXT. IOS - DAY

When Adam arrives in Ios the first thing he sees are a group
of people hanging out by the ferry port.

One of the guys is strumming a guitar and looks friendly
enough so Adam approaches him. He wants to find out the best
places to go and maybe lose himself for a while.

                    LOCAL
          Depends what you're looking for.

                    ADAM
          A typical Ios party night I think.

                    LOCAL
          Do you like dance music?

                    ADAM
          Prefer rock.

                    LOCAL
          Are you going with someone, or
          looking to meet someone?

                    ADAM
          That's a little bit complicated.

                    LOCAL
          How can it be complicated?

                    ADAM
          Can we just say a night out might
          help me think, put things in
          perspective.

                    LOCAL
          Well, I don't know what you need but
          I know a place. Go to the Blue Note
          Bar. It's Scandinavian. Plays rock,
          amongst other things. If you can
          manage a lot of shots in a row they
          give you a t shirt.

                    ADAM
          And a headache the next morning.

                    LOCAL
          Yeah that's free, and guaranteed.

                    ADAM
          Efcharisto, I think.

                    LOCAL
          Pleasure.

Adam's thinking about Eleonore. He's doing some calculations
and writing them on paper. The current attempted scenarios
include the chances of success with her in Sydney,
alternatives to her if they never see each other again, where
Grace makes an appearance, and of course time travel. These
calculations are complex for a Saturday night, and he would
never know if they were viable. He screws up the paper.

                    ADAM
                (To himself)
          Time to find the Blue Note Bar and
          check it out.

INT/EXT. BLUE NOTE BAR - EVENING

The bar is filled mostly with tourists out for a wild alcohol
fuelled Saturday night party.

Adam speaks to the barman.

                    ADAM
          I don't know what I want.

                    BARMAN
          What you want is our speciality.

                    ADAM
          Yes, that will be the thing I want.

                    BARMAN
          And after, the shot!

Adam smiles, has the shot first, then puts the other
concoction on an empty table.

                    BARMAN
               (To himself)
          He goes his own way.

Adam looks at his phone. There is no signal so he goes
outside.

Looking around, the beach at night is just how he imagined
it but the feeling isn't. He's hoping Eleonore's left a
message. She hasn't.

He's been outside for just a few minutes and returns to find
his drink is no longer on that now completely empty table.
The barman gets Adam's attention and points to three women
at the back of the bar who have several drinks in front of
them, including Adam's. The one in the middle is looking
like she's about to sleep or collapse so Adam approaches the
woman on the right. He asks her if she took his drink. She
says she didn't and looks at the woman on the left. Adam
approaches her.

                    ADAM
          Did you take my drink?

                    WOMAN
          I didn't know it was yours. There was
          no one there.

                    ADAM
          Not at that moment. I thought leaving
          a drink for a minute without a
          guardian was safe on this island.
          Obviously not.

                    WOMAN
Well you can have it back then; I
haven't drunk it yet.

                    ADAM
That is undeniably true. If you
really want it you can have it.

                    WOMAN
What is it?

                    ADAM
Try it. I can't say I had you in mind
when I bought it but, la vida es
corta as a lovely friend of mine once
told me. Go on, have the drink, but
tell me something interesting before
I go.

                    WOMAN
Maybe I'll tell you later when you
take me home. Although if you're like
every other man...

Adam doesn't respond. He feels a certain darkness around her,
which reminds him how much he misses the dazzling sunshine
currently a long way east of here.

Her name is Zoe. Zoe seems, by her body language, demeanour,
and words, completely uninterested in Adam, or anyone.
Notwithstanding the entertainment value of this meeting Adam
is remembering some wisdom from Red.

FLASHBACK - INT. - SPORTS WAREHOUSE - DAY

Flashback to when they were on a coffee break while stringing
tennis racquets.

                    ADAM
Red, can I ask you something?

                    RED
Go ahead.

                    ADAM
Why on Earth did you give me the job.
I'm a bit crap let's face it.

                    RED
          When a candidate for a job is
          interviewed, the panel invariably
          knows if someone is unappointable in
          the first 10 seconds.

                    ADAM
          There wasn't a panel, it was just you.

                    RED
          Yep, that might have been a mistake.

END OF FLASHBACK.

INT/EXT. BLUE NOTE BAR - NIGHT

Adam is imagining Zoe as a candidate for the role of his
partner. He is very clear in the first 10 seconds of meeting
Zoe what his decision would be. She definitely would not be
the successful candidate. But he's in the middle of nowhere
and there are t shirts to be won.

                    ZOE
          Bring on the shots!

INT. ADAM'S HOTEL ROOM - DAY

Waking up next to Zoe the following morning, Adam has more
confusion circling his tequila tainted parietal lobe than he
can cope with.

Zoe wakes. They look at each other, with no affection, more
politeness.

EXT. ISLAND - DAY

We see Adam walking Zoe back to her hotel, occasionally
speaking but mostly looking at the scenery. They are now at
Zoe's hotel.

                    ADAM
          I'll leave you here, shall I?

                    ZOE
          What else would you do? You're a man.

                    ADAM
          A good one actually.

EXT. BAR - NIGHT

Zoe has now enticed Adam to go out to drink and dance, over several nights. They both leave the club they're at to get some air for a few minutes. They are sitting on the same wooden bench but not looking anything like lovers.

                    ADAM
          Do you know the song Hotel California?

                    ZOE
          No.

                    ADAM
          You must do! Everybody knows it. It's
          by The Eagles.

                    ZOE
          I don't know it.

                    ADAM
          I like the lyrics.

                    ZOE
          You can sing it to me if you like.

                    ADAM
          Well, I can't sing like Don Henley.
          I'll quote, is that OK?

                    ZOE
          Yes, quote.

                    ADAM
          Some dance to remember; some dance to
          forget.

                    ZOE
          That's it?

                    ADAM
          I think it's quite profound.
                    ZOE
          How is that profound?

                    ADAM
          I was wondering, I was wondering why
          you're dancing.

                    ZOE
          To forget.

                    ADAM
          Yeah.

                    ZOE
          What about you?

                    ADAM
          A bit of both I guess. No, that's not
          true.

                    ZOE
          To remember.

                    ADAM
          Yes.

                    ZOE
          Shall we get another drink?

                    ADAM
          OK.

After some more dancing, Zoe goes to the bathroom and Adam
gets out his notepad again.

He draws Maslow's Hierarchy of Needs. In every one of the
five sections, he has scribbled the letter E.

EXT/INT. HOTEL - NIGHT

Adam is heading home before Zoe. His taxi stops by her hotel
on the way to the airport.

He knocks on her door; she's in the shower. He calls out.

                    ADAM
          Zoe. I'm leaving now.

                    ZOE
          OK. Bye. Safe journey.

Adam leaves and we see Zoe turning off the shower and
looking upset.

She slowly walks to the window with a towel wrapped around
her. Adam's taxi is in the distance.

                    ZOE
             (to herself)
          I think another dance to forget is in
          order.

INT. PLANE - DAY

Adam's on the plane home. He's looking out the window and speaking to himself, in his head.

                    ADAM (V.O.)
          Back to London, retro boy! Yes, you
          don't have an obvious direction, but
          nor did Sid Gautama over two and a
          half thousand years ago and he did
          ok. Get back to what you were always
          good at as a child. When all looks to
          be hopeless, keep on believing and
          things will turn around. Go back to
          the apartment and let things unfold.
          The Universe has your back, be a
          blessing. Have a proper conversation
          with Eleonore. Tell her what's on
          your mind and in your heart. But
          first say thank you to Grace for
          being, so great.

INT. APARTMENT BLOCK - DAY

He unpacks and knocks on her door with a gift he'd searched for on the islands. There isn't an answer. He leaves the gift on her door mat; a packet of Silver Needles White Tea with a note:

"Grace is a wonderful quality, and you have an abundance of it. Thank you for being you, crazy lady.

PS: I'm back if you hadn't realised. Knock on my door when you're home. Love Adam x."

As he's starting to walk back to his apartment, Vincenzo approaches him.

                    VINCENZO
          Are you from Flat 30E?

                    ADAM
          Yeah, how do you know?

                    VINCENZO
          Did you just leave something outside
          Grace's door?

                    ADAM
          Yeah, she's not in.

                    VINCENZO
          You weren't here last weekend were
          you?

                    ADAM
No, I spent most of last weekend
drinking way too much and looking at
the fishing boats on the Aegean Sea.
I'm glad to be back.

                  VINCENZO
You're the person Grace went away
with.

                    ADAM
Yeah. Is something wrong?

                  VINCENZO
Come in for a minute. My name's
Vincenzo.

                    ADAM
I'm Adam, and you are slightly
freaking me out.

                  VINCENZO
Take a seat for a moment, please.
Adam... Grace died, either Saturday
or Sunday. She was alone in her flat
so they weren't sure exactly when
she passed.

                    ADAM
What?

                  VINCENZO
You know she had cancer didn't you.

                    ADAM
     (Clearly shaken)
I didn't know.

                  VINCENZO
We were really surprised when she
told us she was going away for a
couple of weeks. Surprised because of
her condition and also because she'd
only just met you. My wife's been
inconsolable. We haven't been able to
think about anything else. So young,
with that amazing spirit. Such a
wonderful human being.

                    ADAM
          Oh God, it makes sense. How she
          jumped at the chance to go with me to
          the Greek Islands. She knew she had
          hardly any time left didn't she?

                    VINCENZO
          Yes Adam.

                    ADAM
          She's so lovely. Those crazy hippie
          clothes and that head scarf and she
          was really tired after the first
          week, why didn't I see? I was so
          wrapped up in my own world, why
          didn't I see?

                    VINCENZO
          You did something wonderful; you were
          a blessing to her. The fact you
          didn't know about her condition
          probably made her feel like a normal
          person again.
          You weren't looking at her with pity.
          I think that's what she needed.

Adam breaks down.

                    ADAM
          No! Grace. Please don't go! Please
          don't go.

Vincenzo puts an arm around Adam. They stand there for a
moment but it seems like hours.

Adam picks up the note and the tea and makes it back to his
apartment.

INT. ADAM'S APARTMENT - CONTINUOUS

He opens the door and collapses. He spends the night playing
music and crying.

The song we hear is Words by the Bee Gees. The same song he
was listening to when he first met Grace. He sings.

                    ADAM
          "Smile an everlasting smile, a smile
          can bring you near to me. Don't ever
          let me find you gone, cause that
          would bring a tear to me."

Adam falls asleep. The balcony door is wide open.

EXT. FUNERAL - DAY

The funeral is a couple of days later. Lots of people
are there, all wearing brightly coloured clothes as
Grace had requested them to.

At the wake Adam speaks to one of the caterers.

                    ADAM
          Can I ask a favour please?

                    CATERER
          Sure.

                    ADAM
          Could you add something to the hot
          drinks options?.

                    CATERER
          We only have these.

                    ADAM
          Add this.

He gives the white tea he'd bought for Grace and a multi
coloured cardboard sign that says: "Grace's Special Tea.
Lots of health benefits. As recommended by a very special
person. La vida es corta."

A little later the caterer speaks with Adam.

                    CATERER
          That tea is popular. No one seems to
          want anything else.

                    ADAM
          I wish, I wish I'd bought more than
          one packet.

Vincenzo and his wife approach Adam. Vincenzo puts his hand
on Adam's shoulder.

                    VINCENZO
          We should all be grateful we knew
          Grace, for however long it was.

                    ADAM
          Yeah. But if I knew I would have…

                    VINCENZO
          Don't.

                    ADAM
          She told me something. Life is made
          of moments, and when you're looking
          back on your life, those moments will
          allow you the most beautiful inner
          smile. I hope she smiled. But we'll
          never know, will we. I can't stop
          thinking about her being alone in her
          apartment.

                    VINCENZO
          What do you think Grace would want for
          you now?

                    ADAM
          To be happy.

                    VINCENZO
          Yes, so you did get to know her. Now,
          follow her advice.

INT. ADAM'S APARTMENT - DAY

Adam is in his apartment over several days doing as little
as he can in as much possible time. There's a lot of lying
on the sofa, a lot of music, a lot of alcohol. He looks at
his phone and sees a missed a call from Eleonore.

He calls her when he's sure she's working so he can leave a
message rather than speak with her.

                    ADAM
          Darling. I'm sorry I haven't been
          very communicative lately. I had so
          much I wanted to say to you, still
          do. And it's positive, I promise. The
          thing is… the friend I went to Greece
          with, Grace; when I returned I went
          to drop off something at her
          apartment, and I was told she had
          died. I'll be with another neighbour
          later, clearing out her apartment.
          She didn't have family. I hope you
          can be patient for another couple of
          days. I hope the job is going
          wonderfully, of course it must be,
          it's you after all, super- efficient
          and infinitely capable Eleonore. I
          miss you. I love you.

Adam lays on the sofa again. He opens the Southern Comfort
Black, drinking a large glass before going to sleep again.
He has a very vivid dream.

DREAM - INT/EXT. APPARTMENT - DAY

In the dream Grace appears near the balcony. She's very happy
and very healthy, with long flowing hair full of sunlight.
Adam sees Grace and is in temporary disbelief.

                    GRACE
          Hello retro boy.

                    ADAM
          It is you, isn't it?

                    GRACE
          Yes, definitely me. Who else would be
          loitering by the balcony with intent to
          disturb and disrupt your indulgent siesta?

                    ADAM
          But you're…

                    GRACE
          Yes. Not sure for how long I'm here, but you
          know, La vida…

                    ADAM
          Es corta.

                    GRACE
          Indeed it is. But it can and it will be
          wonderful. You just need to focus on what's
          important.

                    ADAM
          I thought I'd lost you.

                    GRACE
          What's important Adam?

                    ADAM
          The heart?

                    GRACE
          A pretty good start.

                    ADAM
          But life's complications sometimes…

                    GRACE
If you let them. There is no fate.
Only choices. You make this life the
way you want it.

                    ADAM
I thought you could help me make sense of
it all.

                    GRACE
It's really not difficult. You need a lot
of love. You're not going to find it in
this apartment, and not sleeping. Drink
less alcohol, more white tea, and follow
your heart.

Grace fades away into the sunlight.
    END OF DREAM.

INT. ADAM'S APARTMENT - DAY

When he wakes up, he visibly really wakes up. Tim is
periodically checking in. He has a key and tentatively
enters the living room and sees a very unkempt living area,
an open Southern Comfort bottle and the balcony wide open.
He looks a little concerned. But then Adam appears with a
towel wrapped around him just having had a shower and looking
extremely bright and positive.

                    TIM
What's occurring?

                    ADAM
I have no idea what day it is, but I
know it's an important one.

                    TIM
Somebody's birthday?

                    ADAM
I'm sure it is, but not knowing the
day or date and consequently not
having bought them a present makes me
a rubbish reveller, don't you think?

                    TIM
Well you're sounding a bit more
like yourself, and you're looking,
better than the apartment. What's
the plan? Is there any sign of a
plan?

                    ADAM
          Yes.

                    TIM
          Is this the part where you make me
          ask a pertinent question?

                    ADAM
          Yes.

                    TIM
          What are you going to do with your
          life?

                    ADAM
          A brilliant question Tim, and only
          one possible answer.

                    TIM
          At last!

                    ADAM
          I'm going to rent out the apartment.
          It's not the best place to be right
          now.

                    TIM
          It's not yours to rent out.

                    ADAM
          Details.

                    TIM
          You're going to illegally rent out
          the apartment?

                    ADAM
          As a beautiful friend of mine once
          said, I'm not a lover of rules.

                    TIM
          Where are you going to live?

                    ADAM
          Wales.

                    TIM
          Wales!

                    ADAM
          Yep, South Wales.

                    TIM
South Wales!

                    ADAM
Is this the part where you repeat
everything I've just said?

                    TIM
Repeat everything...no seriously,
what are you on?

                    ADAM
New, South, Wales. The capital of
which is...

                    TIM
Sydney. You've finally come to your
senses!

                    ADAM
I know, I can't wait. When the first
rent comes in I can buy a ticket and
then I'm on my way. I can stay with
you for a bit can't I?

                    TIM
What did Eleonore say?

                    ADAM
She doesn't know.

                    TIM
She doesn't know!

                    ADAM
Are we back to the repeating the last
sentence game?

                    TIM
Why haven't you told her?

                    ADAM
I thought it would be better to just
turn up.

                    TIM
You don't even know her address do
you?

                    ADAM
I know where she works.

                    TIM
          I'd phone her, now!

                    ADAM
          Yeah I'm sure you would.

                    TIM
          But you're just going to turn up. And
          what if she has a significant other
          with her?

                    ADAM
          I have faith Tim.

                    TIM
          You know what this means don't you?

                    ADAM
          That you're coming round tonight with
          a crate of beers.

                    TIM
          I'll be here at 8.

                    ADAM
          Wicked.

INT. ADAM'S APARTMENT - NIGHT

Later that evening Adam and Tim are at the apartment,
laughing, philosophising, and making inroads into the beers
when someone knocks on the door.

                    ADAM
          Tim, can you get that?

                    WOMAN
          Is Adam in?

                    TIM
          Yeah, can I tell him who it is?

                    WOMAN
          It's Zoe.

Adam overhears and approaches the door

                    ZOE
          Hello Adam.

                    ADAM
          Hello Zoe. Come in.

                    ZOE
          I'm sorry, I'm disturbing you aren't
          I? I should have phoned, not just
          turned up.

                    TIM
               (to himself)
          Phoned not just turned up. Always
          the wiser course of action.

                    ADAM
          Zoe, Tim, Tim, Zoe.

                    ZOE
          Hi. Adam can we speak please?

Tim picks up his jacket.

                    TIM
          Nice to meet you Zoe. Adam, walk
          downstairs with me will you mate.
          What are you doing?

                    ADAM
          I don't know why she's here. She's
          not even local, lives in Brighton.
          I'll make her a tea or coffee or
          something, then get rid of her.

                    TIM
          Man don't mess this up.

                    ADAM
          Trust me.

Zoe has taken off her jacket and is sitting on the sofa.

                    ZOE
          Nice place.

                    ADAM
          Yes, belongs to an aunt. I'm
          temporarily house sitting.

                    ZOE
          Nice.

                    ADAM
          What brings you to Notting Hill?

                    ZOE
I could say I was in the
neighbourhood.

                    ADAM
I find the truth's always a good
option.

                    ZOE
I've been thinking about you a lot
lately.

                    ADAM
Zoe...

                    ZOE
And I really need to talk to you
about something.

                    ADAM
Zoe I'm about to...

                    ZOE
I'm pregnant. You're the father.

                    ADAM
I thought you were taking precautions.

                    ZOE
So did I Adam, obviously, but
nothing's 100%.

                    ADAM
What do you want to do?

                    ZOE
What I'd like to do is see if me and
the father can make an actual go of
this.

                    ADAM
Zoe, we don't even know each other.

                    ZOE
Well we obviously do to some extent.

                    ADAM
I'm about to leave the country. I've
got plans.

                    ZOE
          Oh. Well you should have said that.
          Don't let our little baby come
          between you and your plans. That
          wouldn't be fair would it?

Zoe stays the night in Adam's bed. Adam sleeps on the sofa.

INT. ADAM'S APARTMENT - MORNING

In the morning he wakes to find her making them breakfast.

                    ZOE
          Morning Adam. I know you like a big
          breakfast. Well you did in Greece.

                    ADAM
          Not really hungry at the moment, but
          thanks anyway.

                    ZOE
          Well I've made it now. Can't waste
          food.

                    ADAM
          Perhaps you should have asked me Zoe.
          Or is the concept of seeing what the
          other person wants lost on you?

                    ZOE
              (agitated, becoming angry)
          Oh that's right yeah, hidden meanings
          are your thing aren't they. See I
          personally prefer to be open and
          transparent. I was going to wait
          until after breakfast, but your wants
          and needs seem to have hurried me
          along so here goes. Yes I'm sure
          you're the father, no it couldn't be
          someone else, and oh, here's the
          kicker, I am not going to have a
          termination. There you are, not a
          hidden meaning in sight!

Adam thinks about responding, then decides leaving the
apartment is the better option.

INT. ADAM'S APARTMENT - DAY

Over the next couple of weeks Zoe is living between her house
in Brighton and the London apartment.

Adam is in a daze. He wants to call Eleonore. A couple
of times he goes to dial but stops himself. Zoe comes in
and sees Adam drinking.

                    ZOE
          What are you doing?

                    ADAM
          I'm sure you know. You do it enough.

                    ZOE
          Not in my condition.

                    ADAM
          Here's a question. Why am I doing it?

                    ZOE
          I don't understand.

                    ADAM
          Let's paraphrase Hotel California
          shall we, and change the word dance
          to drink. Some drink to remember,
          some…

                    ZOE
          Drink to forget. I know you'd like to
          forget me, and I know you sometimes
          struggle with reality. So you drink
          as much as you need to, but this is
          your reality, deal with it!

Zoe leaves the room and slams the door.

INT. SYDNEY - DAY

Eleonore and Paul are drinking and clearly loving each
other's company. He moves to kiss her, she hesitates, She
goes to the bathroom and checks her phone for messages.
There are no new massages. She comes back and kisses Paul.

INT. TIM'S HOUSE - NIGHT

Adam is at Tim's house with Olivia.

                    OLIVIA
          Tim's going to be late. He better
          bring home a nice meal, or an
          engagement ring.

                    ADAM
          Tim is a very fortunate man.

                    OLIVIA
          Well I hope he realises.

                    ADAM
          Yes, and in good time.

                    OLIVIA
          I'm sorry Adam.

                    ADAM
          How is it the two most amazing women
          I've ever met are gone for good? One
          to a better place and one to
          Australia, also a better place I
          suppose.
                    OLIVIA
          Why didn't you take precautions?

                    ADAM
          She said she was.

                    OLIVIA
          Was she?

                    ADAM
          She's adamant she was. Do you think
          it could be a mistake?

                    OLIVIA
          What I think, is you can't go on
          hiding from the real world.

                    ADAM
          You, Zoe and Miss Carmen. You'd make
          a great girl group. The Three
          Realities.

Tim comes in, with food.

                    TIM
          Who wants to eat?

                    OLIVIA
          (to Adam holding out her engagement ring finger)
          I'm a bit hungry but I would have
          preferred the other option.

After the meal Olivia goes to take a shower. Adam speaks
quietly with Tim.

                ADAM
Mate, do you remember the first night
you met Eleonore?

                TIM
It was a great night.

                ADAM
Do you remember what she said, about
Olivia, your intentions towards her?

                TIM
It's in hand.

                ADAM
Awesome. I want to write a song.

                TIM
What about?

                ADAM
I don't know, life? Black raspberry
chocolate chip ice cream? You
wouldn't pop round to the apartment
and get my guitar would you? I can't
face another scene with Zoe tonight.

                TIM
You're gonna have to sort it out mate.

                ADAM
I know, just not tonight.

                TIM
Why? You can't put it off much longer.

                ADAM
Tonight, tonight is kind of a special
night.

                TIM
How?

                ADAM
It's the anniversary of the first
night I went out with Eleonore.

                TIM
Oh mate, I'm sorry.

                    ADAM
          She looked so stunning in that white
          dress. And then when she looked at me
          and said "Are we going somewhere or
          am I going with the girls?". And the
          cab driver telling me he doesn't
          think I'm going home. I think that
          was the best night of my life.

                    TIM
          Let's just say the best night so far,
          shall we? I'll get the guitar, but
          don't make it melancholy. How about
          some Rolling Stones, from their best
          period?

Adam smiles and Tim drives to his apartment.

EXT. ADAM'S APARTMENT - NIGHT

As Tim's getting out of his car he sees Zoe with a suitcase.

                    TIM
          Zoe.

                    ZOE
          Hello Tim. He's not here.

                    TIM
          Yeah I know. What are you doing? Do
          you need some help with that?

                    ZOE
          It's OK I can manage, thanks anyway,
          you're very kind. You could do
          something for me though if you don't
          mind.

                    TIM
          Yeah of course.

                    ZOE
          Tell Adam...tell Adam he's free. No
          need to worry about being trapped or
          having to be obligated. He's not
          going to be a daddy. Not with me
          anyway. If he wants the detail tell
          him to look up corpus luteum cyst.
          And tell him, I'm a nice person
          really, just been treated very badly
          by a couple of not

very nice people. I know he wouldn't
want someone like me. We can't all be
completely in control of our feelings
like he is. Bye Tim.

                    TIM
          Bye Zoe.

                    TIM
               (to himself)
          Control of his feelings, oh how well
          you know him.

INT. ADAM'S APARTMENT - CONTINUOUS

Tim calls Adam and he comes back to the apartment. Adam is
now concerned about Zoe.

                    ADAM
          I've got to help her.

                    TIM
          She's going to be OK.

                    ADAM
          But she's on her own.

                    TIM
          Yes, like millions of other people,
          including a certain French lady in
          Sydney.

                    ADAM
          You're right, but I should call her.

                    TIM
          And say what? Hello Zoe, this is
          Adam, not the father of the baby that
          didn't exist, not someone who shares
          even the slightest bit of love or
          affection with you, but how about I
          console you and maybe spend the
          night, oh and by the way I'm madly in
          love with a woman on the other side
          of the world.

                    ADAM
          You're right.

                    TIM
          Twice in one evening. Is it a leap
          year?

Adam unpacks the stuff he'd taken to Tim's and Tim goes back to Olivia. Adam is looking at pictures of him and Eleonore. Flashbacks to his childhood and growing up experiences, good and bad.

He sees an old post it note he'd kept where Eleonore had written "Let me know when you reach 86,400 mon cœur xx"

                    ADAM
               (to himself)
          I have Eleonore. Well grandma, it's
          time for your wonderful wisdom.
          There's no such word as can't.

INT. ADAM'S APARTMENT - DAY

Adam's at home and looking at the clock.
                    ADAM
               (to himself)
          It's 5 am in Sydney. She's never been
          a morning person, she'll kill me!

He gets out his phone to text, then decides to email. Then goes online to find a florist to deliver Eleonore some flowers to coincide with the email.

He sits on the sofa and has a beer… and chocolate…and cherry pie…and now a Southern Comfort…and just a bit more chocolate. He writes Eleonore a message: "Hey shining light. Remember the first time I called you that, at Kelly's that Friday night. I needed several drinks to get the courage to talk to you. I seem to have come full circle because I'm having a couple of drinks tonight in the hope they'll conjure some magic words that will have the desired effect. I'll just get to the point shall I? Probably best.

I've been a complete idiot, for so long now, and I'm going to rectify that. Call me when you read this. I love you. PS: Hope you like the flowers!"

Adam makes sure his phone is charged and curls up with it next to his chest.

Eventually he falls asleep clutching the phone with his choc and cherry stained fingers.

INT. ELEONORE'S APARTMENT - SYDNEY - DAY

Paul is at Eleonore's apartment and about to leave for work. Eleonore is due to leave half an hour later.

Paul leaves and nearly trips over a large bunch of
sunflowers.

He looks at the card. He carefully places it back as it was
and goes to work.

INT. APPARTMENT BLOCK - CONTINUOUS

When Eleonore leaves she sees the flowers and quickly calls
the florist number on the card.

> ELEONORE
> (into phone)
> Can I just check, what time you would
> have left these sunflowers from a
> customer in London? Oh, you start
> work early, what a shame. Merci.

INT. ADAM'S APARTMENT - DAY

Adam wakes and checks to see if he's missed any calls. No
calls but an email:

> ELEONORE (V.O.)
> Mon coeur, I want to call but am in
> back-to-back meetings today. But it's
> important I leave you this message in case
> you decide to do something crazy, like book a
> flight before we speak.
> I have adored you, since even before we met. And
> then we met, and that adoration was replaced by
> affection, and before too long I was completely
> in love with you. I have been completely honest
> about how I feel about you from the start.
> Coming here alone, a new continent, a new
> career, and being separated from the person I
> loved most, do you have any idea how difficult
> this has all been, both emotionally and
> professionally? I have needed you, and for
> whatever reason, you weren't here.
> Adam, I'm seeing someone. It wasn't planned, not
> expected. His name is Paul, I've mentioned him to
> you before. He's been here for me. No one could
> ever replace you. But if you're on the other side
> of the world. I'll call you tonight. 9pm your
> time. Please don't hate me, I couldn't take that.
> Thank you for the flowers, they're lovely.

Adam sits on the edge of his bed in disbelief. He sees an
earring on the sheet. It's one of Zoe's. He calmly gets
washed and dressed, then makes a phone call.

                    ADAM
               (into phone)
     I need to see you. I want to tell you
     how sorry I am. I should have
     supported you when you needed me.
     Instead I was selfish, self-
     obsessed, and any other non-
     complimentary adjectives that I
     deserve to have after my name. Are
     you there? You've gone quiet.

                    ZOE (V.O.)
     I'm here. Where I belong. Don't worry
     about me, I'm fine. It's a nice sunny
     day and I'm going for a walk along
     the beach. We were never going to be
     a long- term thing Adam. Go and be
     happy. Follow your heart.

                    ADAM
     You sound like someone else.
     Something she said in a dream I had.
     It must be good advice if I get given
     it twice.

                    ZOE (V.O.)
     It is good advice. I need to follow
     it myself.

                    ADAM
     I can hear seagulls.

                    ZOE (V.O.)
     Yes, there are plenty here. Take care
     Adam.

                    ADAM
     Take care Zoe.

Eleonore calls Adam at the exact time she said she would.
Adam's phone rings and vibrates, as the cutlery in the drawer
where he's put it, gently rattles.

INT. SYDNEY TOWN - DAY

Over the next few weeks Eleonore and Paul settle into a
routine. When they have to work together Paul stays over, and
most weekends Eleonore goes to his place. The relationship is
a happy one. Everything is very easy. They are the centre of
a vibrant social scene. Greg sees them one evening when
they're out in town.

                    GREG
Hi Paul. And how is my favourite
French Finance manager. Could have
used another F to make that
alliteration a bit more impressive.

                    PAUL
Fabulous, fantastic…

                    ELEONORE
Frightened, at this moment, about
what's coming next.

                    PAUL
I'll get the drinks. Greg?

                    GREG
I'm alright mate. Eleonore, how is
your new life. No regrets?

                    ELEONORE
Maybe one. You know?

                    GREG
I can guess. Is there any possibility?

                    ELEONORE
There are only so many times a question
can be asked, only so much time a person
can wait.

                    GREG
I understand. Well, Paul's a good guy.

                    ELEONORE
He is. I'll always be in your debt Greg.
Thank you so much for the faith you've shown
in me.

                    GREG
Nonsense. We're the winners, having
you here. Now to move on to phase
two. Ousting that horrible sister-
in-law of mine. Are you in?

Eleonore laughs.

                    ELEONORE
Je suis partante à 100%. (I'm 100% up for it)
Yes I'm in!

EXT. STREET - DAY

Adam has told Tim about Paul. Tim is walking home with Olivia and asks her what she knows.

>   TIM
>   Who is Paul?

>   OLIVIA
>   Someone she works with.

>   TIM
>   Is it serious?

>   OLIVIA
>   All I know is, he's a few years older
>   than her, he's confident, worldly
>   wise, financially comfortable…

>   TIM
>   Everything Adam isn't.

>   OLIVIA
>   He's there. Adam isn't.

INT. ADAM'S APARTMENT - DAY

Adam is cleaning his apartment. He is removing any alcohol and putting pictures of Eleonore in the drawer.

EXT. STREET - DAY

It's a very warm Saturday afternoon. Adam takes a walk down to Portobello Road Market.

He wonders around aimlessly, stops at an ice cream/coffee bar.

INT. COFFEE BAR - CONTINUOUS

He orders an espresso and drinks it one go. The woman behind the counter tries to entice him to buy an ice cream too. She is quite flirty with him. Her name is on her badge, Bethany.

>   ADAM
>   What flavours have you got?

>   BETHANY
>   Everything.

>   ADAM
>   Not vanilla. I could never have that.

                    BETHANY
          We don't sell that.

                    ADAM
          Not everything then, as it turns out.

                    BETHANY
          You look like more of a…

                    ADAM
          Black raspberry chocolate chip!

                    BETHANY
          Pistachio.

                    ADAM
          That's not me. Well it didn't use
          to be. I suppose I should try
          something new.

                    BETHANY
          Yes, trying something new is a
          positive thing. Wouldn't you think?

                    ADAM
          You sound like me.

                    BETHANY
          I think we definitely have things in
          common.

                    ADAM
          Maybe. Did a close friend recently
          die, far too young, and your
          girlfriend found someone else, in
          Australia, while another woman told
          you she was having your child, but
          found out later it was a medical
          anomaly?

                    BETHANY
          Not exactly. I was thinking we
          support the same team.

Adam looks down at his football shirt.

                    ADAM
          I'm sorry, Bethany.

                    BETHANY
          It's OK. It's my last day. You might
          be my last customer. It's good to
          leave with someone, different! Back
          to China on Monday.

                    ADAM
          Bethany doesn't sound very Chinese.

                    BETHANY
          My real name is Beiye. It means
          beautiful, resilient, full of life
          and potential.

                    ADAM
          Amazing! I have a strong feeling you
          are all of those things. It's a shame
          you're going back to China. Will you
          be back in London?

                    BETHANY
          If I have a reason to come back.

                    ADAM
          A good reason to go half way across
          the world, that would be something.

Adam is sitting on a stool by the window watching the world
go by but doesn't stay long.

He walks towards the door. Bethany has just taken off her
apron and she is about to leave. She intercepts him.

                    BETHANY
          Don't forget your receipt.

                    ADAM
          I don't need one.

                    BETHANY
          I think you should take it.

                    ADAM
          Honestly…

                    BETHANY
          Take it.

Bethany hands Adam a scrap of paper with her phone number
written on it.

                    ADAM
          Thanks.

                    BETHANY
          Call me.

                    ADAM
          I will. Can I give you mine?

                    BETHANY
          You call me, and I'll have yours. You
          don't want someone clingy do you?

                    ADAM
          I guess, with your travelling plans, it
          will have to be tonight, if you want
          to do something.

                    BETHANY
          It will.

EXT. CLOTHES MARKET - DAY

Adam smiles and wanders over to the clothes market as Bethany
leaves and walks in the opposite direction.

                    ADAM
               (to himself)
          Things are happening.

The market is noisy and bustling and he has no idea why he's
there. A group of rowdy kids are approaching and Adam gets
knocked as they come through.

As he's losing his balance a market trader comes out from
the side pushing a clothes rail on wheels. Reminiscent of an
ancient jousting knight, ice cream instead of lance in hand.
Adam inserts the pistachio fuelled cone into the gap at the
end of the clothes rail and all over an elegant white dress.
The clothes trader is not impressed.

Adam smiles, which makes the trader angry. Adam gets his
wallet out.

As he does this, Bethany's number flies out onto the
pavement, and at the same moment the florist next door
empties a bucket of water into the drain, washing it away.
Adam looks up to the sky.

                    ADAM
               (to himself)
          Things are most definitely happening.

The clothes trader is still looking at Adam.

                    ADAM
          How much?

                    TRADER
          The dress?

                    ADAM
          Yes, the dress.

                    TRADER
          80

                    ADAM
          80! It's second hand!

                    TRADER
          Antique.

                    ADAM
          That's a lot though, 80. I'll give
          you 50.
                    TRADER
          There's a big difference between 80
          and 50.

                    ADAM
          Is this the part where you test my
          maths? I was never any good. Better
          at French. My teacher always said
          what great pronunciation I had.

                    TRADER
          Are you buying the dress?

                    ADAM
          How much is it?

                    TRADER
          Haven't we done this? OK, seeing as
          it has ice cream stains, we'll call
          it 65.

                    ADAM
          Quite a lot of ice cream. Can we call
          it 55?

                    TRADER
          Yes, let's do that. Don't you wanna
          know what size it is?

                    ADAM
          Not really. It's just going in my
          flat. Reminds me of someone. She was
          wearing something just like it the
          night we first went out.

                    TRADER
          Do you think she'd want another one
          just the same then?

                    ADAM
          No, not one just the same. She's
          moved on to something better now.

                    TRADER
          Funny how things turn out isn't it.

                    ADAM
          What?

                    TRADER
          We'd never have met if you hadn't
          bought the ice cream, and if I hadn't
          arranged for my son and his mates to
          push you into my clothes rail, making
          you feel obliged to buy this dress
          that I've been trying to get rid of
          for ages.

                    ADAM
          Yeah, funny how things turn out.
          Hilarious at times. Have you got a
          bag?

                    TRADER
          You might want to get it dry cleaned
          before you…well whatever you're gonna
          do with it.

EXT. STREET - CONTINUOUS

Adam starts to take the white pistachio-stained dress home.
He hasn't got very far when he sees Tim and Olivia coming
out of a local pub. They laugh when they see each other.

                    TIM
          What are you doing?

                    ADAM
          Bit of a long story.

                    TIM
Yep, usually is. Are you alright
mate? We were about to come round to
see you.

                    ADAM
It's alright Tim. You don't need to
check on me. I appreciate it, but I'm
most likely past the jumping off the
balcony stage. Anyway, it's only the
first floor; grazed elbows and knees
haven't got that same dramatic
effect.

                    TIM
Not checking on you mate. We were
going to drop by and invite you
somewhere.

                    ADAM
Is this the part where I have to ask
you a pertinent question?

                    TIM
We're getting married.

                    ADAM
Are we?

                    TIM
Me and this lovely lady. She's less
wayward and far prettier.

Olivia shows Adam her engagement ring.

                    ADAM
Well I might dispute one of those.
Congratulations mate! Olivia, are you
sure you wanna marry him? I am
available, and let's face it a much
more solid, all round, better bet.
Don't you think?

                    OLIVIA
Adam. You know I love you. Just more
like a needy, annoying, little
brother.

                    ADAM
I know.

                    TIM
          Are you psychic?

                    ADAM
          Why?

                    TIM
          Is that a wedding dress?

                    ADAM
          Yeah, this season's must have.
          A pistachio ice cream-stained
          faux Eleonore dress.

                    OLIVIA
          Are you alright Adam?

                    ADAM
          Yes, fine. I am so, so, happy for
          you both, particularly you Tim,
          she's way above your level, you know
          that.

                    TIM
          We all do.

EXT. SQUARE - DAY

Adam says goodbye to Tim and Olivia and heads home. As
he turns into the square he sees Vincenzo and his wife.
They look happy too.

Adam smiles and says hello to them as he's heading to
the apartment. He gets in, puts the dress on the bed and
puts some music on.

                    ADAM
               (to himself)
          Well done Tim. It was in hand after
          all.

INT. ELEONORE'S APARTMENT - NIGHT

Eleonore and Paul have just come back home from a party. She
is a bit tipsy but he is insisting they have another glass of
red wine as a night cap.

Against her better judgement she obliges and while getting
ready for bed opens the wardrobe, glass in hand. She
stumbles, helplessly pouring the wine into the clothes. The
one item that gets the brunt of it is something she hasn't
worn for a while, her white dress.

She breaks down and cries. Paul has never seen her like this.
He tries to console her.

She pushes him away. Paul is shocked.

> PAUL
> Eleonore, it's fine, we'll clean it
> up in the morning. Let's go to bed.

> ELEONORE
> It's not fine!

> PAUL
> I'll do it now, get this wine mopped
> up and take out whatever is stained.
> We can wash it tomorrow.

> ELEONORE
> It can't be washed. It's my
> white dress! Look at it, covered
> in red wine!

> PAUL
> We'll have it dry cleaned then
> darling. It'll be alright.

> ELEONORE
> But it won't. It can never be
> alright. I love it. It means so much
> to me.
> It's one of a kind. I'll never have
> another like it. I love it, so much.

Paul stops for a moment then quietly speaks.

> PAUL
> You're not talking about the dress
> are you?

Eleonore composes herself, softens, and looks into Paul's
eyes

> ELEONORE
> I'm sorry. I'm truly sorry Paul.

> PAUL
> There's been a distant vibe from not
> long after the start. Then the
> flowers. Probably better to know now,
> before too much longer.

                    ELEONORE
          You're a good man.

                    PAUL
          That's what they say. But I'm still
          wondering where the good ending is.

INT. ELEONORE'S APARTMENT - DAY

Morning comes and Paul is leaving the house as Eleonore's
getting up.

                    ELEONORE
          Where are you going?

                    PAUL
          A work appointment, go back to bed.

Eleonore knows Paul wouldn't have an appointment on a Sunday
morning.

INT. PAUL'S APARTMENT - LATER THAT DAY

Eleonore leaves her key to Paul's apartment on his kitchen
table.

INT. ADAM'S APARTMENT - NIGHT

Before Adam goes to bed he hangs the dress on the wardrobe
handle.

INT. ADAM'S APARTMENT - DAY

When he wakes it's the first thing he sees. He stares at the
dress, half smiles and revisits that bravado, just to see if
it still works. But this time, whatever it is that's
"happening" seems to have made the positivity a lot more
authentic.

                    ADAM
          Must get that dry cleaned. It's gonna
          look lovely in the Australian
          sunshine.

INT. ADAM'S APARTMENT - DAY

Adam has been trying to pluck up the courage to call
Eleonore. He has started to dial twice and stopped himself.
The third time, he calls and it rings but goes to voicemail.

                    ADAM
          Eleonore, in a way I'm glad this has
          gone to message. I thought if I
          called and spoke from the heart, you
          know, spontaneity, everything would
          be...Eleonore...you're great at
          stats, so tell me, if I spend all of
          those 86400 seconds every day
          thinking about you, is that a good
          use of my time?
          And what if I can't not do that? Even
          if I was Pierre Augustin Caron de
          Beaumarchais with all those things he
          has to do, I'd probably find them
          dull eventually and be looking for my
          shining light, ma lumière brilliante.
          Because, from the second I saw that
          light I've needed it, needed her in
          my life. What I'm trying to say, what
          I'm trying to say...

Adam is very emotional. Eleonore picks up

                    ELEONORE (V.O.)
          I wish you would say it before the
          message expires.

                    ADAM (surprised)
          Can I tell you to your face?

                    ELEONORE (V.O.)
          Oui, tu peux, you can, you can.

Eleonore is crying.

EXT. ADAM'S APARTMENT - DAY

A   property   let   sign   is   seen   outside   Adam's

apartment. INT. TIM'S CAR - DAY

Tim is driving Adam to the airport.

                    TIM
          Well Ads, finally.

                    ADAM
          Yeah, who'd have bet I'd be going to
          Sydney to be with the most amazing
          woman on the planet? Regan would have
          given that really long odds.

                    TIM
          You're not just going to Australia
          mate, you're going home, to Eleonore.
          Like you should have done a long time
          ago.

                    ADAM
          I'm a slow starter. That's what Miss
          Carmen used to say.

INT. AIRPORT - DAY

Adam's now put his baggage on the conveyor and he's
heading towards departures. He's keen to get on the plane
but takes it slowly so he can spend a little while longer
with Tim.

                    TIM
          Good luck mate, see ya next summer.
          I'm dreaming of a Bondi Beach
          Christmas. I'm sure you know which
          song that comes from.

                    ADAM
          It wasn't the Rolling Stones in their best
          period.

                    TIM
          Give my love to that French Goddess.

                    ADAM
          Not in a million years.

Adam starts walking then turns back.

                    ADAM
          Tim.

                    TIM
          Yeah.

                    ADAM
          Do you think Grace came into my life
          for a reason? So I could be made
          aware that because life is short, we
          need to focus on what really matters.
          And do you think it's all part of a
          bigger...

                    TIM
          I don't know! I don't know.

                    ADAM
          Not much of a best mate are you?

                    TIM
          Go to Eleonore, and make beautiful,
          Australian, babies.

INT. SYDNEY AIRPORT - DAY

Eleonore is waiting for Adam with one of her hands behind

her back. They see each other and both cry.

As he approaches her, she reveals what she is holding. The
poem Adam gave her the day he moved into her apartment, the
lyrics to his song, Another Kind Of Giving.(Song playing).

                    ELEONORE
          I   thought   you   might   need   it.   To
          remind   yourself,   what   you   used   to
          think about me.

                    ADAM
          I need what I've always needed, you,
          nothing else.

SUPERIMPOSE: FIVE YEARS LATER

EXT. ELEONORE/ADAM'S HOUSE -

DAY

Tim, Olivia and their son, are just leaving after visiting
for Christmas and New Year. Adam is saying goodbye yet
again, as they're trying to drive off.

Eleonore waves again as she's getting in her car with
daughters Dhara and Grace.

                    ELEONORE
          Dhara, stop it! Grace, be nice to
          your sister.

She gives Adam an everlasting smile, then melts his heart
with a question.

                    ELEONORE
          Are we going somewhere, or am I going
          with the girls?

                    ADAM
          We're going somewhere.

               THE END

Credits over Welcome To Wherever You Are by Bon Jovi.

Adam, Eleonore and the girls driving, singing and smiling.

Tim, Olivia and their son at the airport going home.

Vincenzo and his wife laying flowers on Grace's grave.

Zoe walking towards her car finding a rose on the windscreen with a note, smiling.

Dhara leaving work meeting up with friends.

Miles and Regan looking at women and giving them a rating.

Teagan packing her things into a box at work. Greg and Paul raising a glass in a bar.

Back to Adam, Elenore and the girls on the beach.